Change
of
Heart

Also by Faith Baldwin
in Large Print:

No Bed of Roses
The Heart Remembers
Arizona Star
Beauty
Evening Star
Face Toward the Spring
For Richer, For Poorer
Innocent Bystander
The Office Wife
The Rest of My Life With You
Rich Girl, Poor Girl
Something Special
That Man is Mine
Twenty-Four Hours a Day

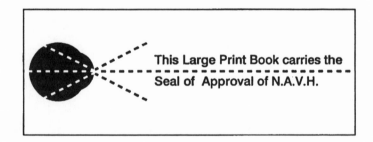

Change
of
Heart

FAITH BALDWIN

Thorndike Press • Thorndike, Maine

Published in 1997 by arrangement with
Harold Ober Associates, Inc.

Thorndike Large Print ® Candlelight Series.

The tree indicium is a trademark of Thorndike Press.

The text of this Large Print edition is unabridged.
Other aspects of the book may vary from the original edition.

Set in 16 pt. Plantin by Al Chase.

Printed in the United States on permanent paper.

Library of Congress Cataloging in Publication Data

Baldwin, Faith, 1893–
    Change of heart / Faith Baldwin.
      p.   cm.
    ISBN 0-7862-1090-7 (lg. print : hc)
    1. Large type books. I. Title.
    [PS3505.U97C48 1997]
    813´.52—dc21   97-1177

THIS BOOK IS DEDICATED TO
A NUMBER OF INNOCENT PEOPLE

To Gonnie, who bore with me patiently and sympathetically during its multiple delivery;

To the editors of Collier's, who were forced to read it too many times and finally gave in — and up;

To my agents, who underwent the same ordeal intensified by my agonized complaints emanating from a distance varying from fifty to three thousand miles, and who, to date, have not given me my notice;

To my typist, who narrowly escaped a nervous breakdown while deciphering the various manuscripts and transcribing same;

And lastly, to myself, who certainly deserves something, however trivial, for having exhibited considerable self-control and proving the triumph of mind over what's the matter.

Chapter One

One sunny Saturday morning last spring, an extraordinarily pretty girl walked into the chaste, costly little shop known as *Chez Mimi* and sat down in a beautiful, low chair expensively upholstered in gray chenille. It was early and a dawn-like hush brooded over Mimi's reception room. Mimi — born Mamie — sold custom-made frocks and hats, lingerie and stockings, and "amusing" accessories. The latter line included costume jewelry at about fifty dollars a chunk of plastic, perfume at a comparable sum per ounce, belts designed by a willowy young man under the influence of bourbon and Dali, and other trinkets. But also, because of the pressure of war times and her patriotic duty, Mimi reluctantly marketed a few ready-to-wears in the interest of those customers whose time was too limited to permit three fittings.

Carol Hillary, waiting quietly for a priestess to come into the outer sanctum, lit a cigarette and surveyed herself in a mirror set into the gray paneled walls. She was not wholly satisfied with her reflection but she might as well be resigned. She had seen the same face and figure with, of course, the alterations wrought by the passing of time, for about twenty-three years. She might as well become reconciled to seeing it, barring accidents, for the next fifty-odd.

She was a moderately tall girl, very sweetly shaped. Her skin was clear, her wide-set eyes were gray, her hair was black and curly. Her mobile mouth was painted a bright scarlet and her little nose was adequate and charming. Her chin, if you looked closely, bespoke either character or stubbornness, depending upon how much you liked or disliked her.

She thought, Dudley likes me in gray.

Her suit was gray, her sables were sable, her silly hat was brown, and she had spent a coupon on the brown lizard shoes which matched her handbag. Her gloves too were brown, as was the cashmere sweater, enlivened by a string of tiger's-eye beads. She wore no other jewelry except upon the fourth finger of her slender left hand, which was decorated with a very large, square-cut diamond, breathing blue and white fire. It was evident that she had not had it long enough to become wholly accustomed to its intimate presence, for she turned it this way and that, admiring it in silence, and with a pleased, small smile.

Smoke spiraled upward from her cigarette, a door opened and a young expensive looking woman with sleek blond hair, a revealing black frock and a quite authentic accent, advanced upon her, hands deprecatory, eyebrows raised. She cried, but not above a whisper, "But, Miss Hillary, I did not hear you come in."

"That's all right, Yvonne," said Carol, smiling, "I'm in no hurry. Is Madame Mimi in the shop?"

Yvonne shuddered slightly. The word shop seemed a trifle crude when applied to the charming, subdued decor. She answered, "But, of course. I shall fetch her at once."

"Thanks," said Carol and watched Yvonne glide away. You would not have known from watching her, fore nor aft, that not many years ago she had cowered in a ditch and listened to the scream and stutter of the diving Stukas.

Madame Mimi arrived, in a tempest. She was always in a tempest. She surrounded herself with an aura of unpredictable temperament and sat quietly in the middle of it, the vacuum at the heart of the cyclone, watching her audience, calculating her effect, and knowing just when to snap out of it before a sale was forever lost. Mimi had been born of an Irish father and a Jewish mother. She was as short and squat as a fabulously well-dressed toad, and like the toad, her eyes were great green jewels, set in the ugly little face.

Carol had known her for a great many years. As a matter of fact, Carol's mother had backed Mimi's venture into her own very lucrative business.

"Darling," said Mimi and dropped her phony accent — it varied these days, depending upon the newest refugee she employed, it could be French, Russian or Czech — "I haven't seen you in ages."

She sat down on a winsome loveseat, upholstered in a brilliant geranium red which gave character to the gray room, and looked at Carol. She said, "You are really a very pretty girl."

"Thanks," said Carol, "so, I came to see if you could make me prettier."

"Gray," said Mimi, frowning, "and brown? Very smart. But a little colorless, isn't it, for you? Better for blondes. With your black hair and your gray eyes —"

"I like it," said Carol firmly. "Mimi, I want a new dinner frock. I don't like the short ones. Long, please, and not too startling. I'm not Jenny."

Mimi smiled widely. She murmured, forgetting that she was talking to Carol, "The so-dear Jenny . . ."

Jenny Davis was only one of the important stage women dressed by Mimi. Mimi dressed — or undressed them all: stage and cinema, social and literary, new money, old money.

Carol said, "It's this way. Mother's coming home . . ."

"It's about time," said Mimi. "Your mother's an idiot. Tearing off to China and the Pacific theater of war, at her age!"

"What has her age to do with it?" Carol demanded.

"And," said Mimi tragically, "with such a wardrobe! I saw it the night before she left. A suit, with a change of blouse and sweater, a stupid little print —"

"At two hundred bucks?" said Carol. "It wasn't too stupid. You sold it to her, Shylock,"

"Well," said Mimi, carelessly, "it was amusing . . . and she said it was all she'd need. That, and a change of shoes, her cosmetics . . . and the sort of lingerie that washes but needn't be ironed, three pairs of cotton stockings and one pair of nylons, and Helen Hillary flies around the world."

"It hasn't hurt her," said Carol. "Anyway, she's coming home next week and there's to be a party and I need a dress."

"That suit," said Mimi, "is three years old and you got it from me, practically wholesale. You are a dreadful girl, Carol. The sables . . . let me see, Helen and Adam gave them to you Christmas before last . . ."

"And a baum marten coat this Christmas," agreed Carol. "Mimi, your spies are everywhere."

"You could afford . . ." began Mimi.

Carol shrugged. She said, "Have you forgotten I took a job a year after I left college? I would have done it sooner but Mother had worn out two secretaries and I pinch-hit. It was excellent experience."

"Oh," said Mimi, "a job!"

"Not that I pretend," said Carol, "to live on the startling emolument which *Foresight* pays its humbler workers in the morgue."

Mimi screamed.

"Control yourself," said Carol, "research department to you. As I said, I don't live on it, I live at home although I'd rather not. But I do like to buy my own clothes and my own cigarettes. So," she added, with her wide, warm smile, "how about a little frock which sells for a hundred and a quarter but which you'll practically give me at a hundred?"

"My dear child," said Mimi, "a hundred and a quarter! Are you out of your mind?"

Carol said, "Quite often, with the most fascinating results. I meant a ready-to-wear, of course."

"Okay," said Mimi, "if you insist." She raised her voice. "Yvonne," she said in a subdued howl, and Yvonne came at the double. "Find Elsa," ordered Mimi, "and tell her I want her to model evening clothes — the ready-to-wear — for Miss Hillary. The white crepe, with the gold belt, the gray and turquoise, the beige . . . Oh, pick out half a dozen and send her in — if she's sufficiently recovered from her hangover," added Mimi in a bitter whisper.

Waiting for Elsa, Mimi and Carol talked. They talked of Carol's mother, who had for so long been considered one of the most beautiful as well as the most brilliant woman in the United States that even her daughter was accustomed to the legend. They talked of Carol's father, Adam Hillary, who had written several best sellers and was currently engaged upon another . . . "I haven't seen Adam in a long time," said Mimi with a sigh. "Is he still the best looking man I've ever known?"

"That depends," said Carol cautiously. "You see, I don't know as many men as you do, Mimi."

Mimi chuckled. She said, "You're lucky."

Mimi had had three husbands, and several runners-up. A great many men find ugly women who are also shrewd, fastidious, intelligent and rich, quite interesting.

Elsa wandered in, with her model's undulations. She was Carol's type, which was why Mimi had sent for her. Her coloring was much the same, and her figure. She was, perhaps, a little more overstuffed above the waist than Carol. Carol's torso produced the effect of gentle, firm curves, but Elsa's looked somewhat crowded.

The white frock was Grecian in design. Carol shook her head and Elsa departed. Elsa's head ached and her nerves were screaming. But there was nothing of the hangover in her measured pace.

She departed and returned, departed and returned. Carol settled for the gray frock. It was the smoky color of her eyes, gray which has both blue and mauve in it. The dress itself was beautifully cut and the slim waist was encircled with a van-colored sash, turquoise, cherry, fuchsia.

"I'll try it," said Carol.

Mimi was present at the trying. She nodded, well satisfied. There need be only a slight alteration, she said. She watched Carol turn in front of the mirror and suddenly screamed, to the honor of the fitter, poor

14

wretch, who was tired, overworked and had four children to support. She screamed:

"Carol, what's that on your hand!"

Carol looked at her hand as if it weren't her own. What a dope she had been, she thought, not to take it off and put it in her bag before Mimi arrived.

"It's a ring," said Carol mildly.

"You drive me nuts," said Mimi. "Of course, it's a ring. It's quite a ring," she added, seized Carol's hand and regarded it, for a considerable length of time. "And was that a Christmas present too, from Helen and Adam, or did you go without your lunches to buy it?" she inquired.

Carol said, resigned, "Look Mimi . . . I just got it, last night. I haven't told anyone and God knows I didn't mean to tell you. I'm waiting until Mother comes home to make the announcement."

"Darling," said Mimi, "I swear I won't tell a soul!"

"You," said Carol affectionately, "are a platinum plated sieve."

Mimi looked hurt. Her jewel eyes misted. She said:

"I'm a worthless woman, Carol, and I'd sell my grandmother's body if the price were high enough. But I don't betray confidences." She remembered the fitter suddenly

15

and looked down at the meek, small woman who was busy doing things to the hemline of the frock. "You, Bella," she said, "you may scat."

The fitter scatted.

"Now," said Mimi, "who is he? Not Pete Tomlinson?"

"Pete," said Carol, "was a passing fancy. He is now on a battleship somewhere."

"Howard Carey?" asked Mimi. "I saw your picture with him, taken at the Stork or somewhere, last year."

"Howard's in the Air Corps —"

"Well," said Mimi, "for heaven's sake, who!"

"Dudley Lennox," Carol told her.

Mimi's mouth fell open and stayed that way. When she had the power to close it she said feebly, "You mean to say —!"

"Listen," Carol interrupted, "get me out of this dress and I'll tell all."

Mimi obliged and Carol sat down in a chair and took a cigarette from a crystal and silver box on the low table nearby. She said, "I've known him, slightly, for years. He's quite a friend of Mother's and Father's and I've seen him at the house, and here and there. But of course he seemed years older —"

"He is," said Mimi, "not that it matters."

16

"He's thirty-six," said Carol.

"Or thereabouts," said Mimi. "I've known him for ten years. He used to come in here with —" She broke off and Carol grinned. Carol said, "Don't spare the horses. I know all about her anyway."

"Oh, well," said Mimi, "in that case . . ."

"In that case," said Carol, "we won't discuss it. When I went to work for *Foresight* I just walked in, cold, asked to see the Personnel Manager, told him what I thought were my qualifications and got myself a job. I didn't get it through Dudley. He didn't know I was working on the magazine until he came into the department one day and saw me. He nearly dropped dead."

Mimi said, "Then he didn't know you very well." She looked at the girl and reflected. No, of course she wouldn't use Hillary influence to get herself a job.

Carol said after a minute, "Well, that's all. It was a year ago and I've seen a lot of him since."

"What does the family think?" Mimi inquired.

Carol rose and stepped into her skirt. She said, "I wouldn't know. Mother likes him, quite a lot, I believe. I don't think Father does especially. He's a little suspicious of every man who isn't in the war — principally because he himself would like to be."

"But he's fifty," said Mimi, startled.

"I know, yet he's tried everywhere and everything. He could get a desk job, of course, but he doesn't want that. He still thinks he can fly — he hasn't forgotten the last war, he's still living in it."

Mimi asked, "But why *isn't* Dudley Lennox in?"

Carol said, "He has a knee injury — from football, and a slight heart murmur. Also he owns and publishes *Foresight*, and that's considered pretty important. It isn't old, as news weeklies go, but it is just about tops. He owns a motion picture outfit, Mimi. He had intended to go into competition with March of Time. That sort of thing. Instead, he makes propaganda shorts for the Government. He's in Washington a lot, and has, besides, a sort of hush-hush advisory job. I don't know much about it."

Mimi asked, "When are you to be married?"

Carol shrugged. She said, "I don't know. Autumn, perhaps." She added, smiling, "It's hard to set a date, I never know when Mother and Father will be around at the same time — what with her war corresponding, lecture trips and all that — and he, well, of course, he's always off somewhere, lecturing too. It's quite a merry-go-round. The only person who stays at home is Aunt Agatha."

"Tell her," said Mimi briskly, "that it's time she came in for a fitting."

"I don't know why," said Carol, "she always wears the same dress, short for day and long by night. Black."

"It isn't the same dress," said Mimi, "it's merely another just like it." She smiled. She said, "I wish you happiness, Carol, for I don't know anyone who deserves it more."

Carol said, touched, "Thank you, Mimi."

Mimi added, "And when it's time to select your trousseau —"

Carol laughed. She said, "I knew that was coming. All right — everything *Chez Mimi.* And now I must run — hairdresser," she said vaguely. "Please, Mimi, can you get the dress to me early next week if possible? And we haven't talked price."

"No price," said Mimi with a shudder at her own madness, "it's an engagement gift."

Carol hugged her. She said, "Nope, you'd have insomnia for six weeks. Just cut it down to my size, Mimi — and when I know definitely when Mother returns I'll call you. The party wouldn't be complete without you, and you know that you and Jenny Davis are the only women Mother can stand . . ."

She kissed Mimi's cheek lightly and, properly attired, left. Mimi went into her strictly utilitarian, rather shabby office which no client ever saw, took a box of small brown cigars from a desk drawer, lit one, sat back in her swivel chair and thought. She thought about Carol Hillary, whom she loved, and about Helen Hillary, whom she reluctantly admired. She thought about Adam Hillary. He was one of the few men with whom Mimi had ever fancied she could be in love. She had not been in love with any of her husbands, including the current one, nor for that matter with any of her lovers — ditto. She thought of Jenny Davis who was the brightest single star on the musical comedy stage, and one of the world's most enchanting women. Jenny Davis had been in love with Adam Hillary for a good many years. And he, it was assumed, with her.

Why didn't he divorce Helen? thought Mimi — and God knew he had plenty of grounds, discreet as she was — was one of life's major mysteries.

She pressed a button, a harried minion appeared and Mimi said, "Bill Miss Carol Hillary for the gray frock . . ." she looked at the price tag which she had brought with her. It read, one hundred and fifty dollars. She said, sighing, "One hundred."

"Gray," said the secretary, "which gray?"

Mimi said with impatience, "There's only one. It's called 'Before Twilight.'"

The secretary scurried away. Mimi relaxed. This was a screwy business but it paid off. She wondered when the party would be. She wondered if Helen had aged. Any other woman would age. Rocketing around the skies, smelling the smoke and blood of battle. Helen was in on everything. She had been blitzed in London and torpedoed in the Atlantic. But nothing aged her. Nothing left its mark; not the success, nor the money, nor the adulation nor the excitement, nor the weariness of travel, and none of her reputed, and generally reputable lovers. But — *had* they been lovers? thought Mimi, who was interested in her friends' diversions. If so, Helen hadn't been in love. That's what ages you, thought Mimi, sagely, keep yourself detached and you haven't a new line in your face when the time comes to say goodbye and good luck, or, goodbye and good riddance.

She turned her thoughts to Carol. Carol was a completely real person, by herself. Surround her with parents and she became unlikely. It wasn't possible that between them they had produced her. Mimi flirted a little with the idea that perhaps they had not; or at least, that Adam hadn't. But that wasn't

21

any good. Carol looked like Adam, she had his dark hair, his gray eyes, and his chin, in a feminine edition.

She hoped that Carol would be happy with Dudley Lennox. Lennox was as eligible a man as you could find nowadays. He was rich and orphaned. He had never been married. The lady with whom he had visited *Chez Mimi* in the past had not been Mrs. Lennox. She had been Mrs. Somebody Else.

Yvonne came in. Importunate clients waited, so Mimi put out her cigar and assembled her accent. This morning had cost her a good deal, she reflected. Her profit on "Before Twilight" would be some forty bucks instead of ninety. But you could afford a gesture, for sentimentality's sake. And Helen had been responsible for *Chez Mimi*. To be sure she had been repaid with interest, Mimi's heart's blood and crocodile tears, but the obligation remained. And Carol.

She sailed into the reception room and looked severely at a plump blonde whose husband had seen the war coming. New money. She could smell it a mile off. She smiled inwardly. The fifty dollar gesture would return to her, a thousandfold.

Chapter Two

Carol met Dudley Lennox for luncheon, after the hairdresser. She was a little late and he was waiting for her in the small lounge of the French place where they had often met during the past months. He rose as she entered and looked at her with pleasure. He took her hands and murmured, "Mind if I kiss you — now?"

"Very much," she said sedately, but her heart beat a little faster. She thought, I am in love with him, he's wonderful.

He was not a very tall man but he was well and compactly built. His hair was as dark as her own, but there was a salting of gray in it. His face was controlled and dark, his teeth very fine, as were his hands. His eyes were hazel and quiet under heavy brows. There was strength about him; you felt it at once, discipline and vitality. He could be, she knew, entirely ruthless. She had seen this quality in operation more than once and had heard repercussions of it. He could also be extremely generous.

Lennox was a clever man. In the face of very hard competition he had built the reputation of his magazine within the last decade. It was not his only interest although since the war he had concentrated much time, thought and money on it. He had inherited a fortune and doubled it. He had been mentioned several times as a likely candidate for important Government appointments, and if he had wished to enter politics he could have made another name for himself. But he was not interested in appointments or politics. He was far more powerful in his own person, and controlling his own interests.

They went directly into the dining room, as Carol never drank at luncheon. Dudley's short Scotch was brought to the table and he ordered. He did not consult his fiancée. He had no need to do so as he had spent almost a year discovering her tastes in food, drink, entertainment, amusement, and diversion. After six months of this interesting research he had asked her to marry him and she had refused. He had gone privately to her mother.

He remembered that day, a cocktail lounge, a quiet corner, an early appointment. Helen was between a luncheon lecture and a radio broadcast. He remembered thinking how beautiful she was and wondering why he wasn't in love with her instead of with her daughter. He remembered her saying:

"She's quite young for her age, Dudley. Give her time. Personally, I approve of you, if that's any advantage, which I doubt, as Carol and I rarely see eye to eye, despite our natural devotion. She's stubborn — rather," Helen had added thoughtfully, "like her father. She hates being swept off her feet by anything — a person, an emotion, a decision. I suppose she gets that from her great aunt, as it's not like Adam, nor like me. And she loathes publicity."

"What has that to do with me?" he had asked, laughing.

"Oh, you," she said lightly, "you're spectacular. Carol doesn't like that. It's a reasonable reaction, I dare say, from her father and me. She should of course be taking an active part in the war — I have repeatedly urged her to join up — in one of the women's branches of the service. But she said, 'I couldn't be Private Hillary. I'd just be the Hillarys' only child.' That's why she works at Red Cross and at being a Nurses Aide instead of doing something more exciting . . .'"

Well, that was six months ago. He had bided his time, no other man had come along, or none who could trouble him, and last night he had taken Carol to dinner, straight from the office, produced the ring

25

and his second proposal. This time, she had said, yes.

He said, "You are looking very pretty, darling."

"I bought a new frock," said Carol, "at *Chez Mimi.*"

Dudley said, "Mimi's an interesting woman — I used to see something of her."

That was rather nice, she thought. He didn't say, "Who on earth is that?" nor did he go to the other extreme and say, happily, "Yes, of course, I used to buy clothes for Mrs. Somebody Else there — I have good taste and her husband never knew the difference. He thought she ran them up on an old loom."

Dudley had told Carol about the woman, years his senior, who had been his mistress from the time he was twenty-six until two years ago. She had been discreet, charming and grateful. He would have married her, during the first few years of their association, but she had considerable common sense. She would grow old, perhaps not gracefully, and Dudley would not. Besides she was fond of her husband, she always added, plaintively.

When they parted Dudley was thirty-four and she was forty-eight. It had been time. There were no recriminations and all in all it had been a satisfactory intimacy. It had kept him from marrying the third girl in the front row or the debutante daughter of Mrs. Gotrocks or one or another of his pretty secretaries.

Now, he was marrying Carol. Which reminded him of something.

He asked, "How about June?"

Carol said, "That's too soon."

"When," he demanded, "won't it be too soon?"

She said restlessly, "Please don't rush me, Dudley — This is fun — just as it is. And I want to keep on with the job for a while. I like it."

He said, "After we are married you may keep on, too, if it pleases you. Or with any job you prefer."

"That's sweet of you," she said, "but not sensible. Anyway, I don't believe it. You wouldn't make a place for me if I were not qualified for it. That's not how you run your organization"

"No," he agreed, "but if it would amuse you, a place can be found for which you would qualify."

Carol shrugged. She said, "I have no career ambitions. When I marry I expect to be the sort of wife you read about and rarely, if ever, see. I expect to run your house —"

"Houses," he said.

"Plural then," she corrected herself, "with the help of competent servants, if such are to be had —"

"Could we snitch your mother's couple?" he inquired.

"I'm afraid not," she told him.

"Which is why," he said, "the Connecticut place is closed, the Palm Beach house and the shooting shack in North Carolina — and why I live at an hotel."

"And like it," she said.

"Well, yes," he admitted. "We could, for a while."

Carol said, "I wouldn't mind. I just want to be with you, Dudley." She smiled at him and his heart tightened. He hadn't intended to fall in love, not like this. Oh, some day, of course, an attractive, suitable wife who appealed to his five senses. But he hadn't expected nor wanted this headlong insanity, this compulsion.

She went on, flushing under his ardent regard, "And I expect to have children. Several of them."

"Good," said Dudley, "but first, wouldn't it be a sound idea to set our wedding date?"

She said, "I've always liked October."

"October first," he said. "That's settled."

She said, after a moment, "Half the people in the office suspect. Not that I mind. But perhaps it was foolish of me to wait until Mother gets home. I mean, we're not a conventional family —"

"You are," he said, "you and Aunt Agatha."

She said smiling, "Perhaps I'm a throwback. Anyway, as soon as she's home and settled. Perhaps — " she looked at him, "I thought at the party . . ."

"It sounds all right. Who's giving it?"

"No one actually gives it," she said helplessly. "I mean — Mother comes home and there's a party. At our house. I suppose we give it. But, I sometimes think that she brings it with her."

"What do you know about the boy she's bringing with her in addition to the party?" he asked curiously, "this infant Major — Miles Duncan?"

"Why, nothing," said Carol, "should I? And is she?"

"There was something about it on the ticker today.

He's the kid who shot down all the Zeros in the national debt," Dudley explained. "There hasn't been much released. Just that he's on his way home. White House decoration, a long leave, all that sort of thing. He's twenty-three or four and a Yankee — from Portland, I believe. No parents, brought up by a grandmother who died last year.

"But what," she demanded, "has this to do with Mother?"

"My information was," he said, "that they're coming in on the same plane . . ." He laughed a little. He said, "Of course she'll collect him. She's been collecting heroes for a year now. Before that, promising playwrights, novelists, poets, painters and just plain *promising*."

Carol flushed, slightly. She said, "Well, some women collect spoons and some like Windsor chairs and I met one last week who collected harness brasses!"

"Ten to one he's at the party," said Dudley.

Carol laughed. She said, "I won't take it. It's probably a sure thing."

"I met your mother," said Dudley thoughtfully, "about ten years ago — she was the loveliest woman I had ever seen. She still is. If I hadn't been otherwise occupied, she might have collected me."

"I'm glad she didn't," Carol said serenely, "as I was bound to encounter and want you for myself. Which would have created a situation, without appeal."

He said, "Well, don't blame the baby Major if he sits around all dewy-eyed and just looks at her. Can you imagine what it must be like, sweating it out over jungles, sitting in the briefing room waiting — coming back again with half your friends on the one way list, and sweating it out some more — and then suddenly be headed for home, and with a woman sitting beside you who looks like Helen Hillary, and who *is* Helen Hillary? That's powerful medicine, darling."

"I suppose so," said Carol. She wasn't especially interested. There were thousands of heroes, most of them unsung, and only one Helen. Ever since Carol had been old enough to observe and to think, ever since she had sensed the antagonism between her parents, and their several ways of compensating themselves for it, she had neither judged nor condemned them. She believed herself to be civilized and modern — whatever that meant. She believed that her parents were entitled to live their lives as they saw fit. If she did not much like the way they lived, if she felt smothered and steam-rollered because, now and then she got in the way, well, it was her hard luck but not her fault. Nor theirs. People are as they make themselves. Some of her philosophy came from her great aunt — a spinster lady who had lived with the Hillarys since Carol's birth and who had brought up Carol's mother — but not her tolerance. Carol's tolerance was her own and she had learned it the hard way.

She smiled at Dudley.

"You know," she said, "I like you a lot."

"Well, thanks," said her fiancé, raising an eyebrow.

"Well, of course, I'm in love with you too," she said, "but then I've been in love before."

"As much?" he inquired and waited, concealing his very real anxiety.

"No, of course not," she said, very sweetly. "But liking you makes it all quite wonderful and right." She raised her eyes, very luminous but a little troubled. She said, "I haven't been sure, Dudley. There are times when I'm not quite sure, even yet. And I must be, dear.'

He said, "You will be."

She smiled and after a minute she said slowly, "I think so. You see, liking you as much, and loving you too — there — there is a *security* in it . . ." she halted. "I can't explain exactly," she added, like a child, "but it's something I've never felt, something — real, like the ground under my feet."

He took her hand and held it. He said, "Darling . . ." He said, "Why must we wait until October?" And thought, She's right, of course. What child of the Hillarys could feel secure? Not this child, certainly. One perhaps, who was selfish and willful, and motivated only by egotism, one as beautiful as Helen, as brilliant as Adam. Because he was. Much more so than Helen — which burns her up. Such a child might feel security in that lunatic menage, but not Carol. Never Carol.

He said, gently, "I shall love you all my life."

Chapter Three

The big plane which carried, among other important passengers, Helen Hillary and Major Duncan, came sailing through the misty pearl and azure of a spring morning in Manhattan. The towers clustered together in the Wall Street district, the pinnacles of midtown seemed rootless and topless, veiled in the mystery following the dawn. And Miles Duncan spoke to Helen:

"It's beautiful," he said, "and I'm glad I'm seeing it with you."

She said, smiling, "Coming home is always an adventure— and your homecoming especially so."

He said, low, "It wouldn't have meant much — without you."

"Nonsense," she said, "an old woman!" She looked at him. Her eyes were as nearly black as the human eye may be. She looked rested and refreshed although they had battled head winds, and had been delayed, as early in the flight the plane had been forced to turn back. Her flawless skin was unlined except for laughter stars around her eyes, and a concentration mark, delicate as the imprint of a bird's foot, between her brows. If those brows and her lashes were slightly darkened, if her glorious red-gold hair had been brightened with rinses, Miles didn't know it. As a matter of fact, rises were hardly *de rigueur* in the places in which Helen Hillary had recently been.

He asked, jealously, "Will your family meet you?"

His blood, thin from the tropics, ravaged by fever, but hot with youth, cooled uncomfortably. It seemed incredible to him that this woman had a husband. Incredible, indecent, and heartbreaking. Incredible too, that she had borne a child — her body, small and firm, weighed no more than a hundred pounds. He knew, because one night, when they were in a strange and perilous place, the sky had come alive with death, and he had picked her up in his arms and stumbled, with her, to a shelter. He had crouched there in the darkness, feeling her warmth and vitality beside him, and sensing, too, her utter lack of fear. He was not fearless. He had lived too long with fear and uncertainty, with death and disaster as his companions. He had shuddered, when he heard the slow whine, the abrupt detonation. But Helen had put her arms around him and said, "There, there," as one says it to an anxious child. He had not resented it, for she understood. She had seen, she had taken her beauty, her clear mind and her fragility into the dreadful places, so, as much as a woman could know, she knew . . .

Helen said, "Heavens, no, I loathe public reunions. Adam and Carol have sense enough to stay at home. And, of course, my aunt."

The aunt was clear enough to him. Helen had told him about Agatha Stuart, spare and uncompromising, "the backbone of the family," who was almost as legendary as Helen herself. Helen had said, "People — especially interviewers — insist upon calling her a New Englander, specifically a Bostonian. It infuriates her, as she was born on lower Fifth Avenue and hates New England — particularly the cooking. Sorry, Miles, I forgot you were from Maine!"

But this child, Helen's daughter, she was vague in his mind. He thought of her as colt-thin, with freckles, with braces on her teeth and pigtails. Which was of course absurd, as Helen had told him, upon the day they encountered one another, under distant skies, that she had a daughter who worked on *Foresight*, "— a lovely creature," she had said, "and as unlike me as possible."

Well, that was right. No woman could look

like Helen Hillary, she was unique.

There had been nurses, they were grand gals and he had loved and appreciated them, they were worked to the bone and marrow, they took their chances with the other soldiers. They were swell. But he hadn't been able to romanticize them, he had been too ill for one thing and they had been too busy. Also there'd been girls whom he still remembered, crazy, exciting girls whom he had known briefly, for a day, for a night, on his infrequent leaves. There were girls back home. Fun and games, though he hadn't had much time for them. Now, in a sense he had no time at all.

When he had first taken Helen's hand in his own, he had felt as if he had dreamed, and dreaming, had died. For there was no such woman this side of Paradise — cool, and poised, smiling and ageless (yet she had told him her age almost immediately) — utterly bereft of most of the feminine trappings. He had stood there gaping at her, like a schoolboy, knowing too well what she was seeing in return, a tall and lanky kid, in a uniform which no longer fitted him, a kid far too thin, sallow with fever, jumpy with nerves. . . .

Her little suit he would always remember — she wore it now — the serviceable, well worn tweed, soft as a kitten's ear, and neutral in color. Her hair had been brushed into shining natural curls, short and like a halo, her lipstick — which she carried in her pocket — had been as bright as challenge, fresh as sunrise, gay and courageous as a flag.

Now he said, "I suppose I sha'n't see you," but not believing it.

"My dear," said Helen Hillary, "you'll see me much too often. I wish we could put you up but my colossal house has no guest rooms. As a matter of fact, no guest in his right mind would want to stay in such a squirrel cage. Adam and I come and go. Carol has her own life. Aunt Agatha is the only stable factor — together with the servants who have been with us for years, poor souls. But after you've had a rest at the hotel, and seen the press —"

"Must I?" he asked, in alarm.

"Child, of course," she said in her warm caressing voice. She went on, smiling, "Then, you must come to us. There'll be a party of sorts."

"Party?"

"Not really, just a few people of whom I am fond. Later, we'll dig up some pretty girls for you and see that your leave is really made glamorous."

He commented that dug-up girls sounded

repulsive, like mummies, and added that he wasn't interested — in girls.

"You will be," she prophesied. She looked swiftly about the plane and then put her hand briefly over his. She said, gently, "I've been thinking of what you said the other night. You mustn't even think of it. It — was just the romantic circumstances and the fact that I'm the first civilized female you've seen in a long time."

He was silent, his jaw set a little sullen. He thought, ~~God damn~~ her husband, ~~God damn~~ the twenty years she was on earth and I not there. ~~God damn~~ everything!

They had fastened their belts for the landing. And Helen sighed. She said, "Everything will be so flat after this — after China, and the rest of it." Her long eyes slid around to his and his heart pounded against his thin ribs.

The time of their arrival had not been made public but there were people waiting, on the field, people who had been there since dawn and earlier. Miles, following Helen from the plane, saw them, the tight, smiling, waving knot of humanity, and knew that his hand shook and he wished for nothing more than to turn back and plunge into the anonymity and safety of the plane. Helen sensed this, at once, took his hand, and held it.

Smiling, she said, "Steady," in a low, vibrant voice and her touch, her smile was all he needed and he went forward with his tall head held high and his face set in its concealing mask.

He was twenty-four. He had been a Major at twenty-three. He had left college for combat. He had seen plenty. He had done more than his share of killing. He had watched the skies for planes which did not return. Some of the best guys he knew were dead. He had been lucky. He was home, all in one piece. Except for the shakes, nightmares and a couple of mental skins lacking, leaving him raw and sensitive, he was all right. He was going to have another decoration, the highest. He was going to the White House. He had been given a leave, then he would be sent to instruct somewhere. He might even lecture to women's clubs and men's luncheon meetings, he might even sell bonds, and patriotism. By God, he thought, I'm a hero — and the hell with it!

The reporters closed in around him and Helen. There were other men there, and presently he met them — first a man named Whitney, Helen's publisher, a good looking guy, Miles thought and watched him kiss Mrs. Hillary, with evident pleasure. He had been afraid to kiss her. He had wanted to

40

until he ached, but he had been afraid that she would suffer it, compassionately and then laugh at him gently. Now another man was kissing her, he was short, dark and ebullient, Jacobs, her lecture manager. . . and yet another, gray-haired, with thick shoulders and a lined face, Hanson, her agent.

Miles stood there and answered the reporters' questions. He stood there while the battery of motion picture cameras were trained upon him and then on Helen. He was docile, he opened his mouth and said the words which were recorded upon the sound track. Tomorrow, perhaps, a million people would see him move, speak and stiffly smile, upon the newsreel screens. He stood there and took it and it was worse than the angry chatter of machine guns. If Helen could take it, so could he. But he felt lost and forlorn and utterly alien to himself. The interlude was over. The journeys, the stopovers, the wings spread in flight, and Helen talking of herself, deprecatingly, detached; Helen talking of him — that was over, all over.

Suddenly, savagely, he wished himself back again, back in the makeshift hospital, back on the baked field, back in the briefing room. He wanted no part of this. He wanted no part of quick moving, quick speaking men who asked questions, no part of assured, well dressed, overage gentlemen who claimed Helen Hillary as their own, who took her in their collective arms and kissed her with their collective mouths.

He thought, Where do I go from here?

He went to a hotel. Everything had been arranged for him. He didn't know how, exactly or by whom. But Helen could manage things, she could manage them it seemed from jungles, from beautiful, stinking, devastated cities, she could manage them from planes and probably, from lifeboats. She said, in the car which belonged to Frank Whitney, "It isn't big and you'll like it. It isn't," she added, "too expensive either."

He didn't care about that. The pay piled up and there wasn't anything you could do with it except gamble, and he was always lucky. He didn't lose, he won. Sometimes you paid fifty bucks for a fifth of whiskey, but you won it back on the roll of the dice, or the turn of a card, the next night.

She added, "And it's close to us. I thought you'd like a quiet place."

He said sincerely, "You're marvelous."

Frank Whitney looked at Major Duncan. He quirked an eyebrow. He said dryly, "You don't know how marvelous." He thought back a number of years. He thought of a manuscript which had reached his desk, and of the woman who had written it, and who had come to his office. He thought of a lot of things. Well, water under the bridge, and why he still remembered, why he had not forgotten his painful pleasure, the continuous excitement and slow disillusionment, he wouldn't know. He thought, I hope to God she leaves the poor kid alone.

Aloud he was saying something about — if the Army were agreeable and if the Major would give a little of his time — a book, a thin, factual book? Such books were bound to sell. Also and apart from their commercial value, they were important, they were contemporary history. It didn't matter, he said, over Miles' protests, that he felt he couldn't write. All he had to do was talk. There were plenty of good people who could do the writing. He, Whitney, wished to be in on the ground floor. He looked at Helen. He suggested, upon an inspiration which was amusing, yet a little reluctant, because he knew what he was doing, "Now, if *you'd* write it, Helen?"

She had a good deal to write, on her own. She had lecture and radio engagements to fulfill. But she spoke at once. She said, "I'd like to, it would be a privilege."

Whitney watched Duncan's face. Hooked,

he thought. Well, bully for our side — poor devil. \

Helen was explaining in her casual way. She was saying, "He can't really get away from us, Frank, until his orders come through. And he has no people here."

"Nor anywhere," said Miles suddenly. "Maybe I'll take a run up to Portland to see my friends. I don't know. My grandmother's dead, the house has been sold. I —" he shrugged, "I don't feel like going back. Not just yet."

Whitney suggested that the Major must know a raft of people in New York.

"Oh, girls," said Miles vaguely, "when I was at Amherst — weekends in town, New York, Boston. Most of them are married now, I dare say. As for the fellows . . ." His voice drifted off. You didn't have to ask him to go on — they were tramping through mud, they were dying on beaches, they were raving in hospital wards. They were establishing beach heads, building bridges, standing watch on ships, they were slogging through their basic and advanced, they were out on maneuvers, on mountain terrain or in the desert. They were in the brig or the guard house. They were flying planes, or learning to fly them. They were scattered all over the face of the globe and its waters.

When they reached the hotel, Helen said, "You know the address. Take a taxi. And we'll expect you early. About, shall we say, nine — before the rest of the people come?"

Miles stood on the sidewalk and the spring sun shone on the bare, untidy head. His very blue eyes, much too old, much too embittered, looked straight into her. He said, "I'll be there."

Frank asked, "Am I invited?"

"Weren't you?"

"Oh, sure. Carol 'phoned. She wouldn't leave me out," said Frank, "we're friends. But I like it from the horse's mouth."

Helen laughed. She leaned out of the window, her brilliant hair curling from under the edge of the tight, becoming turban. "There's always a party when I come home," she told Miles.

Frank Whitney grinned. He said, "You create one, darling," and Miles Duncan could have strangled him for the easy endearment.

The fact was that because it was easy, it was all right. There had been a time when it had meant something, when it had been natural to say the little lovely word, yet difficult — because of Adam, because of Frank Whitney's wife. That time was gone.

Driving toward the Hillary house, "Good trip?" Whitney asked.

"The best," said Helen. "Exciting."

"Well, we'll hear all about it," said Frank, "via ether waves, printing press, and probably Braille."

She said indifferently, "You don't like me much any more."

"No, dear."

Helen laughed, "That's all right with me." she said.

"You're an agreeable woman," he said. He added, "That's quite a kid you brought home with you. I hope you don't hurt him too much."

She said, with asperity, "Don't be absurd and likewise banal. He's twenty-four years old. I could have a son his age."

"Or older," said Frank, "if you'd started young enough."

"Didn't I?" she inquired. "There's Carol, as evidence."

He said gravely, "I meant that, Helen. I'm warning you."

Helen lit a cigarette. She said, after a moment, "I understand Miles and boys like him."

"Maternally?" he suggested. "Well, God help him!"

She flushed, faintly. "You have," she suggested, "a nasty mind."

He nodded, complacently. "Nastier than you know," he agreed. "But I'm not worried, mind you, from what you term the banal angle. You can dish it out, darling, but you can't take it. I speak as one who has been present at the feast. It was all papier-mâché. It looked pretty but it stilled no hunger. I am not in the least concerned with the corruption of our young Major's gaunt flesh — but with the corruption of his spirit. Because when an essentially cold woman remembers her age, faces it, and decides that her maternal instincts have not been wholly satisfied —"

Helen interrupted, viciously, "I'd rather you didn't come tonight," she said.

"Oh, but I shall," he told her happily. "Carol asked me. If I don't, it will cause comment. Besides, whatever I do, you can't retaliate. I have you under contract."

The car stopped. This was the Hillary house, on the East Side but in a neighborhood not too fashionable. It was old, big, and brownstone. Helen had remodeled it into a series of suites. The people who lived in it could live as privately as it pleased them to live. They could encounter in a communal dining room or drawing room. It was one of the most interesting houses in New

York and it sheltered — when they were together — one of the most interesting families — or so the legend ran.

Chapter Four

Carol was dressing for the park. The house, which had been quiet, sedate and a little sleepy, had come alive. It was still quiet but you could feel the tension and excitement. It was always like this when Helen came home. Marta and Ole felt it in the kitchen and Cresson, Helen's invaluable personal maid, vibrated with it as a hummingbird vibrates in the sun. Helen's brace of secretaries, who had met her at the house and had remained for early dinner, had departed but you could still feel their exclamatory emotions, the jealousy of one another which animated their flat, middle-aged, female breasts.

Carol put on the gray gown and looked at herself in the mirror. Mimi had kept her word, it had come in time, and was worth whatever that horse-trader had charged for it. It was almost indecently becoming in an entirely unspectacular way. She leaned closer to the glass and with a bit of tissue removed a tiny lip rouge mark from her square, white teeth. No use, she thought, all the looking in the world can't give you long black eyes and hair neither red nor gold . . .

She picked up the jade pendant. Helen had blithely smuggled it home— a bit of jade for Carol, another bit for Aunt Agatha. It was very good, heavy and cold and satin smooth, the gem jade, emerald jade. It hung on a slender chain, it was not carved, not tortured into intricate faces and figures. It was money in the bank.

She dropped it in the jewel box in the dresser drawer, took from the box Dudley Lennox's ring and put it on the correct finger with considerable satisfaction. This too was authentic, solid and real. But it was not exotic; it had not been smuggled. It had not been bargained for — "The last thing they owned, and they had once been extraordinarily wealthy," Helen had explained, "and of course the Chinese inflation is simply fantastic. So I bought it, for practically a song — it will become you, it will make your eyes green,"

Carol didn't want green eyes tonight.

This had been quite a day. Carol had stayed home from the office and between them, she and Aunt Agatha had made the final arrangements for the party. Aunt Agatha had said, sighing, creaking a little in her old joints, "I don't know why we do this. Wouldn't it be more sensible if your mother just came home, and, after a while, went to bed?"

"She'd hate that," said Carol, "and expects this — yet every time she's as surprised and pleased as a child. We can't *not*, darling, she'd be hurt even if she didn't show it."

She remembered at this point, that her father had wandered into Agatha's utilitarian little office downstairs and commented, "Baked meats again, return of the prodigal. The old routine."

Carol turned the ring on her finger. She had said nothing yet. Too much excitement, people coming and going, more reporters, photographers, and the secretaries buzzing around, their hands filled with letters, and telegrams. Flowers, and weary delivery boys tramping up and down. A field day for Miss Hayes, she thought, Miss Spry, Miss Muller and all the rest, when Helen Hillary came home from the wars.

She wondered what her mother would say when she told her of her engagement. Some of the anticipatory pleasure was lost because she believed that Helen would be pleased. Not that Helen had ever urged Carol to marry. She had often said, "Much as I want you to be happy and settled, Carol, I resent the thought that such a transition might — will, in all probability — lead to making a grandmother of me." Yet, thinking it over she hadn't appeared too downcast, her eyes had shone and she'd added, "Well, maybe it would be fun."

Lots of fun, Carol had thought at the time — big cocktail party and a new man and Helen crying, "But, my dear, good soul, I'm a *grandmother!*" Or the introduction from the lecture platform or over the air. . . "this beautiful and brilliant woman who combines homemaking with a remarkable career, a woman who, though the outstanding political and war correspondent of her sex, has found time to marry, to create a home, who has brought up a charming daughter, and whose chief interest lies with her home, her husband, her daughter, and, believe it or not, her grandchild!"

Nuts.

Carol frowned. Helen liked Dudley. Adam, she thought, did not. But it was hard to know what her father thought of anyone. He was always detached, and an onlooker. He had tremendous charm when he chose to exercise it. He hadn't exercised it on Dudley. He had known him of course for years but only recently had he seen much of him. He had put it this way: "How come that after eons of avoiding his type, I fall over a man like the foresighted Lennox every time I enter my happy home?"

Naturally, they disagreed; they disagreed upon politics, and other things. Adam had a vast contempt for what he called bright young men with a talent for expediency

It didn't matter, Carol thought. She was marrying Dudley. Her mother wasn't, nor her father. She wanted all he represented. She wanted a solid life. She wanted a life with roots. She wanted security. She wanted everything she had never had and now had found. She would not let it go.

So, she would tell her parents before the guests arrived and leave the furor and the public announcement up to them.

She wondered briefly what Major Duncan would be like. She thought of the young men who had infested the house ever since she was a child, young men who, her father re-marked, crawled out of the woodwork. All types. The football players, the brawny boys with scant small talk who often knocked over the teacups or spilled cocktails. The intellec-tuals, a little balding, even at an early age, with the completely snob-slant of their cult; the gifted young men, with too apparent vi-rility, or too little. The boys who liked to decorate boudoirs or design hats. The boys who were recovering from an unfortunate love affair. The boys with too much money and those who lived on rye bread, ham sliced thin, and cokes, but who had dinner coats and an appetite for dry martinis and good buffets.

Latterly, before Helen's excursion into the Orient, the boys had turned up in uniform. Many were similar to, or a reasonable facsimile of, those who had come, and gone, before. Some were different — kids from small towns, from far states, kids who were seeing a woman like Helen for the first time.

Carol wondered just where the Major fitted in, or did he?

Cresson pattered up the stairs, the agitated White Rabbit to the life, and knocked on the door with her hard little knuckles. She was a thin woman and her long nose was perennially rosy. She had been with Helen ever since Helen could afford her. She had traveled with her until wartime conditions made that impossible. She adored her. All the servants adored her. Helen was lenient. She issued her orders, she expected service. She got it. She paid high wages, she employed good doctors, she gave vacations when it did not inconvenience her. She was lavish at Christmas. Now and then she confided in her employees. She never confided anything which mattered, she was never without dignity nor familiar, but it made them feel important. It was the same with the secretaries who slaved for her and hated one another. The only person, thought Carol, who doesn't like her is Miss Perdon.

Perdon was Adam's secretary. She was in love with him. All his secretaries had been. So he had taken to selecting them with care — Perdon was fifty and looked it.

Cresson came in. She said severely, "Mrs. Hillary wants to know if you are ready, Miss Carol. Some of the guests have arrived."

Carol jumped, and looked at the clock on her dresser. Was it so late? She had been sitting here, day dreaming, remembering, and now the guests had arrived and she had not told her parents of her engagement. But, she excused herself, when had she had a minute with the house in such utter confusion? The maternal gift of rare jade had been presented in the presence of, practically, a multitude — you couldn't say, "Thanks for the jade, and how do you like my diamond?"

Well, she would wear it now, and let the chips fall where they may, only there weren't any chips. This diamond was flanked with chaste platinum and blazed by itself in a special glory.

Carol rose. She said, "I'm so sorry, Cresson, I quite forgot the time." She looked down at the smaller woman, "You look tired," she said.

"I'm dead on my feet," said Cresson, well pleased, "all that running up and down!"

Carol went to the door. She looked back at her room. It was big, and a little shabby. She had steadfastly refused to have it redecorated. She loved it. It was private. She had, beyond it, a smaller room which served as a study, and a bath. Aunt Agatha's suite was a replica except in decor. Aunt Agatha's furniture was strictly from Victoria.

Cresson slept in the attic, surrounded by plentiful chintz, air and light, her whole being concentrated on the bell wire which ran from her room to Helen's, two floors below. Marta and Ole were housed in the English basement, beyond the dining room, kitchen and pantry. Between them, with outside help, they managed the household.

Carol asked, on the landing, knowing Cresson's little ways, "Has Major Duncan come? Have you seen him?"

"I got a look at him from the stairs," reported Cresson, "he's a very tall young man, and he seems peaked."

Carol went down to the drawing room. Dudley wasn't there. She had said, "Don't come till lateish, darling — it may give me a chance to tell them." But the chance hadn't offered itself. Or was it that she could have manufactured one and hadn't even tried? She told herself, with exasperation, But, that's silly of me, I can't keep it private, unless we elope and we can't elope because Dudley would hate it and it would mean more publicity in the long run. Besides, it would hurt Aunt Agatha.

Her step was soft and unhurried. She could see them, and before they looked up and saw her. It was a portrait group.

The drawing room was very big. It was done in pastels. The rug was a faded Aubusson, strewn with undying roses. The mantel was white and fine, above the fireplace. Adam Hillary stood there. He was an outsize man — he was enormous, tall and wide but, miraculously, not heavy. He had less gray in his black hair than Dudley Lennox. He wore a square brown face and gray eyes.

Helen was minute beside him. She wore leaf green, a long dress. She had emeralds in her ears and on her hands. She looked as if all her life she had done nothing but sleep late mornings and go to hairdressers and specialty shops, as if she had never seen an unhappy nor a horrible thing — it was difficult to realize that she had looked on blood, had heard and smelled and touched death;

57

difficult to realize that she had sat in a life-
boat for eleven hours while a man died at
her feet, despite all she tried to do for him.
Because she did try. That wasn't newspaper,
that was Helen. She could strip the clothes
from her body, she could shelter and warm
a dying man, with her garments and flesh,
she could listen to his delirium, and nurse
his sickness, she could hold him in her fragile
arms, she could close his eyes.

Frank Whitney was thinking this, standing
nearby. He was thinking, Give her her due,
she's beautiful, she's a bitch and she's the
bravest woman I know. Why?

Carol saw Frank, she saw Jacobs, and
Hanson, she saw a radio commentator. She
saw Mimi, too, ugly as sin, in the smartest
frock of the season, blazing with remarkable
and authentic jewels. She saw young Duncan.

He was standing next to her mother, and
Adam was talking to him. He answered but
his eyes were intent upon Helen. He was,
Carol saw, too thin, and very tall. His lack
of flesh made him look taller. His uniform
might have been pressed, but he hadn't had
time to have it cleaned. Evidently, he traveled light. The uniform didn't fit, it hung
on him.

He looked up. Beneath the fair brows and

58

the straight tow-colored hair, which had recently been cut, his eyes were very blue.

Helen followed his regard. She cried, "Come in, we've been waiting for you. And what in the world has happened to Aunt Agatha?" She turned to Miles helplessly, "My child," she said, "has no sense of time. How she holds a job is more than I can fathom."

"I do it with mirrors," said Carol. "Aunt Agatha's in conference with Marta, I think."

She held out her hand to Miles. He took and shook it, hard and briefly. His eyes were stunned. He said to Helen, "But I thought —"

Adam laughed. He was very entertained. He had been entertained ever since Miles' arrival, ever since he had greeted him and seen, beneath the courtesy and deference, the stark hostility. Courtesy because I'm his host, deference because I'm an old man, and also by now, if Helen hasn't already told him, he knows I'm considered a big shot, in my limited sphere. But he hates my guts. So she's done it again. Set her down anywhere and she'd do it. Put her in Tibet and she'd have a Lama eating out of her hand and serving her steaming hot tea complete with rancid butter and probably uncut turquoises. Well, thought Adam, amused, he hasn't seen a white woman in months, or anyway not one who's counted, so this is like seeing all the wonderful women in the world in composite. The other Helen, and Beatrice and the rest. The beautiful and damned. It won't hurt him, that kid's tough, underneath, maybe it will afford him an escape.

Helen asked, "Why incredible?"

"But," he murmured, his eyebrows knitted, "I thought your daughter —"

Carol was used to this, and mechanically helpful. She said, "Of course you thought I was nursery size. I don't blame you."

Miles looked at her with gratitude. He didn't like her because she, like Adam, intruded, she spoiled the landscape. Landscape with figures. One figure. Helen's. Little and light and ageless. But here was a tall girl, cool, too poised, a hard girl he thought. Good looking, he decided warily in her way, if not, of course, like her mother. Like, perhaps, her father, whom he distrusted and disliked — big, brutal, intellectual — How a woman like Helen — ?

Helen moved closer and looked down at Carol's hand. She said, *"Carol!"*

Carol shook her head. She suggested, "Perhaps this isn't the time or place . . ."

But Frank was there and Adam was saying

something under his breath. He was saying, "Damned if she hasn't done it." And Mimi was crossing the room with her duck's waddle and crying, "Do you mean you haven't told them?"

The door chimes sounded. Ole opened the door, there was a brief murmur of voices and Dudley Lennox came in. He was like safety made visible. Carol moved toward him, at once, put her hand on his arm. She looked, her father thought uneasily, both lovely and defiant.

He said, before Helen could speak, "Hello, Lennox, I fancy you know everyone here except Major Duncan — who together with your future mother-in law, has just returned from the wars."

Chapter Five

The shouting and the tumult died. Helen kissed her daughter, Adam kissed her, everyone kissed her. Dudley's hand was wrung from his wrist. Adam pulled bell cords and Ole appeared and the shakers and decanters already on the bar wagon were supplemented by champagne in buckets of ice.

Mimi said proudly, "I knew!"

Helen looked at her coolly. She liked, as Carol had said, very few women. Mimi was one. Mimi amused her and was, certainly, no competition. She "adored" a number of sprightly, fashionable females, with whom she had little in common beyond biology but they admired her extravagantly; and she was an affectionate sister to all the famous women of the generation — those whose signed photographs lined her workroom above the book shelves, the *Who's Who* women of all the Americas, England, China, France, Scandinavia.

There was one woman however, reputedly Helen's closest friend, whom she most cordially hated.

Adam strolled over to Dudley, his champagne glass in his hand. He said, "I don't often enact the heavy father. But you'd better be all that fathers expect of their daughters' husbands. Or else."

Dudley grinned.

"We've had our differences before, but on this, we see eye to eye," he said.

Adam contemplated him. He didn't like him. He admitted his charm, and his qualities of imagination and initiative. He thought, Yet he isn't for Carol. That was maudlin. Why not? How does any man, especially the girl's father, know? He thought, I always believed she was like me.

He put his hand on Carol's shoulder and closed it, hard. He said, "If it's okay with you, it has to be with me."

He loved his daughter very much. He hadn't, he thought with his usual clarity, lived up to the obligations of loving her. Or, had he? When the first time he suggested to Helen that a divorce was the most decent solution of their situation, she had pointed out to him that because of Carol a divorce wasn't indicated. It would be more decent, for Carol's sake, to work it out another way. Two ways, really, hers and his. How long had it been since they had lived together, as the euphonious phrase runs? Nearly fifteen years, he thought.

Helen cried, "But this is all wrong! Where in the world is Aunt Agatha?"

"We'll go find her," said Carol, took Dudley's hand and escaped from the room. She said, as they went downstairs, "That was a little sudden."

He held her fast on the stairs, on the narrow tread, turned her to him, kissed her. He said, "I liked it."

"Mother is already writing the announcements to the press, mentally," said Carol.

He said, ruefully, "I suspect, darling, that she wasn't very pleased."

"You're wrong," said Carol, "she likes you, she approves."

"I mean — we stole a little of her thunder."

"She can afford it," said Carol, laughing. "Do come on, Dudley."

He asked, "Couldn't it be sooner than October first?"

She shook her dark head. "Not one minute," she said firmly, "it will take me that long to get used to the idea."

They went on down, and found the small tables in readiness, the hearth fire blazing, the flowers looking like spring in crystal. Aunt Agatha was there with Marta. She looked up as they came in and said crossly, "We aren't quite ready."

"We didn't come to eat," Carol explained, "but to tell you we're going steady. I waited until Mother came home to announce it and then thought I'd delay the procedure until after the party. But I had on my ring —" she exhibited it, smiling — "Mother saw it, and simultaneously Dudley was wafted through the doorway. Father saw him and the world-shaking secret was divulged. I wish you'd been there. I thought you'd see Ole bringing up the champagne and would follow —"

Agatha said, "I've been busy with Marta in the kitchen." She drew Carol close, inclined her head and kissed the girl's cheek. She held out her hand to Dudley and he shook it, feeling that a great-auntly embrace would be fitting, but had not the temerity to suggest it. Agatha patted Carol's hand, said, "That's a very lovely ring," and added, "of course I've been expecting this."

"I hope you approve," said Dudley, tentatively.

"If Carol loves you, of course," Agatha answered.

"Is that a quibble?" he inquired.

Agatha regarded him. She said, "When engagements are announced the interested bystander merely prays and hopes. I hope, for instance, that I live long enough to see you married for, say, ten years. It's unlikely," she added practically, "but it would be gratifying. Marriages don't set over night like aspic, nor take quickly, like vaccinations."

Carol laughed. She put her strong young arms around the spare, seemingly brittle figure of her great-aunt, and hugged her. She said, "You know you're relieved to see me settled."

"I shall be, when you are," said Agatha austerely. She untied her white apron and announced that she would come upstairs and drink one glass of champagne, although it was poison to her system and her joints. "And I want a good look at that flying boy," she added, as Dudley and Carol followed her from the room. "What's he like?"

"Oh, young," said Carol, carelessly, and Dudley added, "Too young, I think, to look as old as he does at times."

Upstairs, Miles, curling his hand around his cool, smooth glass, was talking to Helen. He said earnestly, "This must have been a shock to you —"

"It was, rather," she admitted, "although I had seen it coming and am very happy about it. Yet I suppose it's always a shock to a woman to realize that her daughter is to be married — even though she plans marriage for her practically from the cradle."

He said, wanting to shelter her, wanting

66

to help, "I wish they had waited until another day. You just came home. This is your party," he said, awkwardly. He added, "You look so tired."

Helen said, "I'm never tired," and looked at him with brief anger. But her sparkle came back, the dimples tucked into the corners of her mouth were on parade.

She was however so tired that her knees were paper, and her bones, putty. She thought wearily of the long hours ahead, people, food, drink, chatter, noise, confusion, and longed for the wide bed in which she slept alone, for hot milk, a sleeping pill, the shades drawn and the spring night drifting through the room. But she never admitted fatigue, which was one way to combat it. She knew, as she took excellent care of herself, that a night's sleep and forgetfulness would restore her fully. She did not expend herself in trivialities as other women did. She hoarded her amazing strength for amazing achievements. She conserved herself, and gave little. She took, much. Therefore this boy was important to her. She could take from his youth, his adoration, his basic vitality. She could draw upon it as one draws upon a limitless bank account.

If you give nothing and if you take freely you remain young. If you surround yourself with youth, it is as a flame, and you do not grow chilly, shivering in anticipation of winter.

Dudley and Carol returned with Agatha and other people came in — an attaché of the British Embassy up from Washington, a columnist, a radio executive — the room filled gradually and when Agatha had wiggled her eyebrows twice at her niece, Helen said, "We won't wait for Jenny — it's a late curtain and she has a million curtain calls to take. She'll understand if we go on down."

They trooped downstairs and helped themselves at the buffet and bar and carried plates and glasses to the tables. It was informal and lively, the food was excellent, and as varied as ingenuity could accomplish, and rationing permit.

Helen managed deftly. She put Miles Duncan at the table with Dudley and Carol and the columnist. She said, "Nursery table," and smiles at Miles, to take the sting from that. She knew better than to surfeit any man. Feed his hunger lightly and he remains semi-starved.

Miles looked at his plate. There was too much on it. He grinned at the columnist, whose name was Merkin, and remarked that it wasn't much like field rations.

They talked of war, or rather Merkin

talked and Miles listened. He would rather not, but he was courteous. No one in this room, he thought, knew anything about war except Helen Hillary. He found himself saying so in a rather loud voice.

"And my father," said Carol. She watched him, the effort it was for him to eat, she saw that he drank rather too much yet it did not seem to affect him. She was tabulating him, his too-thinness, his nervousness, apparent in the fact that he talked a lot, and then not at all, that he spoke too slowly or in bursts of speed, the words tripping at one another's heels.

Miles said, "Your father?"

Carol said, "Of course. He was instructing in English at a Midwestern university during the last war. He married my mother —"

"Who was," interrupted Merkin, in bored recitative, "the child prodigy of her time, and a Junior in his class . . ."

"Yes, I know," said Miles, "she told me." Merkin raised an eyebrow and grinned at Dudley whose face, as behooved one soon to be a member of the family, remained impassive.

Carol said, a spark of anger in her eyes, "And then he went to war. He flew with the Lafayette Escadrille, and later with our own small forces . . ."

"Came home," supplemented the columnist and yawned widely, "went back to teaching, wrote a book which shocked the faculty into a coma, and then after you were born, Carol, tore off to the well-known capitals of Europe, to report currents and undercurrents." He dropped an eyelid at Dudley. He said, "You can read it in *Who's Who*."

Helen came up and put her hand on Miles' shoulder. She said, amiably, "Don't believe a word that Jerry Merkin says. He lies by the book and it is his livelihood."

"He wasn't," said Miles, shortly, "telling me anything I don't know — as yet."

Frank Whitney, reloading his plate, wandered by. He said, "Jerry, you are always looking for respectable items — although you rarely use them. How about this one. Major Duncan is going to write me a book. At least, he's going to talk me one and Helen will write it."

"Well," said Merkin, his eyebrows climbing, "that's news."

Miles said, uncomfortably, "Look here, I didn't promise —"

Helen kept her hand on his shoulder. Its light pressure increased. She said, "If you don't want to, you needn't."

"Nonsense," said Dudley, "it will sell a

million copies. It may even outsell *Without Mercy.*"

Without Mercy was Adam Hillary's last book. It had hit the jackpot. It had had a remarkable press, critical prestige and man-in-the-street popularity.

Miles said, with an effort, "But you can't talk about things . . ."

"You should," Dudley advised, "it gets them out of your system."

Helen took her hand away. Miles missed it. He felt alone. He looked alone. And Helen said, gravely, maternally:

"You sha'n't force him, Frank, nor any of you."

Carol thought, But she's forcing him. . . .

Miles grinned suddenly. His face altered, was young and gay, the face of a boy who had never heard machine guns, and flack, who had never seen the Zeroes at Six O'clock.

Carol thought, But he's just a kid . . .

He said, "Of course, I'll do the book, Mr. Whitney — only I'm not much good at talking."

"Helen," said Whitney, "will take care of that — she could extract water from the desert, revelations from the Sphinx, and extra gasoline from the OPA."

Helen smiled, faintly. She looked at Miles'

plate. She said, "You aren't eating. . . ."

Immediately he was ravenous. She drifted away, and Miles attacked the cold turkey, the ham, the Newburg. If he consented to do the book he would be with her — for hours and hours, for days and days. What a dope he had been not to realize that!

When Jenny Davis came in, Ole brought her downstairs, although it was hardly necessary. She knew her way around this house and her place in it. Adam rose, and Helen, they advanced upon her, they kissed her, one upon one cheek, one upon the other. It was a pretty picture.

Jenny was small and dark, and lovely. Her frock was white, her mouth deep rose. Her eyelids glistened, her creamed and powdered skin was delicate and fine. She was thirty-five or perhaps thirty-eight. She didn't look it. She had taken the fortress ten years ago and held it against all comers. Hollywood fished for her, with a golden line and a golden lure, but she would not rise to it. She was comfortable as she was. She would photograph well, she was slim enough and there were tricks with soft focus and gauze. But she liked her flesh and blood audiences and the aura which rose from them, the feeling that she could hold them, all of them, in the palm of her hand. The musical in which she was starring had run since January and would go on running. It was a handsome production, the story, lyrics and music fashioned for her, as personally as Mimi designed her clothes. Jenny could sing a little, and dance a little. More, she could read lines, she could even act. But even if she couldn't, it wouldn't have mattered. She loved the people out front, and they loved her in return.

Jerry Merkin embraced her with fervor. She was, he said loudly, his dream girl.

Everyone's dream girl.

She hadn't, she'd often said, a teaspoon of brains. Well, that didn't matter either. She had all she would ever need. She was sweet, unspoiled and exciting. She was also very unhappy.

Helen brought her to Carol's table and Miles and Dudley rose. Jenny flipped her hand at Dudley and smiled at Carol. She cried, "Why don't you ever ring me up?" Miles, standing grave and tall, was presented. Jenny took his hand. She said, "It's an honor, Major," and her eyes filled with tears. They were quite genuine, and Miles was embarrassed, but Jenny was not. Dudley said, "Congratulate me, Jenny . . ."

"On what?" asked Jenny, and, in answer, he raised Carol's hand and held it. The diamond caught the light.

Jenny's eyes spilled over. She put her arms around the younger woman. She said, "If he doesn't make you happy I'll — I'll haunt him."

"It's an interesting but difficult proposition," said Dudley, thoughtfully.

Adam materialized and said, "Jenny, here's your plate." He pulled a chair up to the table and ordered, "Woman, sit down." He looked at the plate with pleasure. He said, affectionately, "She eats like a horse."

How long has the affair gone on? thought Merkin; good Lord, it was before my time on the *Globe.* Why don't they do something about it?

Jenny rose, presently, her glass in her hand. She said, "I want to give a party for Carol, and Dudley. Sunday — at my place. Eight-thirty till breakfast. Everyone's asked." She turned and smiled down at Miles Duncan. "Especially you," she said, "please."

She thought, I wonder how Adam likes the engagement. Well, she would know soon. He told her everything. He came to her for those qualities which he found nowhere else. For the qualities of warmth and listening and consolation. These she had given him ever since they had first known one another, when she was understudying a great English star,

74

shortly after he and Helen had agreed to go on living under the same, expensive roof.

Carol was the stumbling block. Carol. She should hate Carol but she loved her. It wasn't Carol's fault.

Chapter Six

Carol's engagement to Dudley Lennox was duly announced. The office furor died, the social exclamations. The photographers and caterers, the furriers and lingerie shops, the jewelers and decorators, sent their little pleas, telephoned, made the customary gestures. The date was fixed for October first and life resumed its more or less normal aspect.

What was normal to the Hillarys would be abnormal to almost any other household. Helen went off to lecture, returned to broadcast, and to outline her own book. Miles went to the White House and was decorated. He went to Portland and walked the familiar streets, and shook familiar hands and looked into familiar eyes, yet felt as if he had never before been in this city. Because he hadn't been, not really, not as he now was. He spoke haltingly at men's luncheon clubs. He sold bonds. Then, he came back to New York, on a train which seemed to crawl. Because only in New York could he feel alive and real, when he was with Helen Hillary.

He came to the house and sat with her in

her workroom. The secretaries were banished, as a deterrent. Helen had a marvelous shorthand of her own. No one but its creator could read it, not even John R. Gregg.

The workroom was big and sunny. It contained a little electric grill. Helen could make tea or coffee there, without benefit of Marta. Her bedroom was beyond her dressing-room-bath. Adam occupied the same type of suite in the front of the house. Helen overlooked a sizable backyard, which had tulip beds and a green, green tree.

She could give Miles only an hour this day, two hours that. He sat in a deep chair, slumped against it, and talked, or was silent. She listened and made her fantastic notes. This would be quite a book, she thought with a spark of envy, far better than her own. Her own would be adventure and excitement, great names and dramatic effects. She would be part of its pattern, a bright thread twisting through, holding it together, giving it color, charm and life. But the things Miles told her, painfully, in the sunny morning hours or toward the soft-footed dusk, were terrifying and warning, they were real and naked, they had no charm, they held no adventure.

He did not talk only of the book and what must go into it. He said, one warm day, when spring had forgotten her virgin reluctance:

"You aren't happy."

"Oh," she said lightly, "what's happiness? I've been very successful, I have friends, and a life which satisfies me."

He said doggedly, "No."

Helen smiled. She said, "My dear boy — !"

"Don't say that!" he shouted at her. Then he said,

"I'm sorry. It's just —" He looked at her miserably.

"Why wasn't I born," he demanded, "twenty years earlier?"

She said, "That's sweet of you, and I believe you mean it. But if we were of an age, you wouldn't have liked me. When I was the age you now are, Carol was four years old. Her father was in Europe and I was here in New York with Aunt Agatha and my baby, determined to have a career." She laughed. "I dare say I was an unpleasant little wretch."

Never unpleasant, simply — determined. Any means. Any ladder. Forget the means, kick away the ladder.

She added, reproachfully, "I've produced half a dozen attractive girls for you, Miles."

He said restlessly, "I wish my orders would come through."

When they came, she would lose him. She couldn't afford to lose him, not yet.

She said, "I don't believe you like girls!"

"Don't let a psychiatrist hear you," he warned her, "or I'll be 4F, suddenly. Sure, I like 'em — but you've spoiled me."

She picked up a paper knife from the desk and bent it in her strong small fingers. She said, "Now, if it hadn't been for Dudley, you and Carol —"

He said, "Carol?" in alarm.

"You don't like her, do you?" asked Helen softly. "I watched you dancing together at Jenny's party. You looked very grim."

He said, "I'm a little afraid of her. She laughs at me, underneath."

Helen said, "She isn't impressed — is that what you mean? But you don't demand that people be impressed, do you? Although it's pleasant when they are."

He nodded. He said, "I suppose you're right. Asinine, isn't it? Hero stuff. When I think of the better guys —" He added, "No, that isn't it. I feel something else — that she doesn't trust me, perhaps, or she doesn't like me any better than I —" He broke off and said, in astonishment, "That's a damnable thing to say."

She said, "I can detach myself from the fact of my maternity. Carol isn't easy to know, nor to understand. She's like her father in some ways. But, mostly, very like herself. Dudley, however, understands her."

"I think," said Miles, "that she's making a mistake there. Not that it matters to me. But it would," he said, "to you."

"Very much," Helen agreed, gravely. "Yet you're wrong. He's right for her, Miles."

"Good," said Miles heartily, "then I needn't worry." He hesitated. He suggested, "Maybe she resents — us?"

"Us?" repeated Helen, coolly.

"Well," he explained, "she must know how I feel about you. Everyone must. Coming here," he added, "I like less and less. Mr. Hillary is most kind," he said, with bitterness.

"Adam likes fliers," said Adam's wife. "He fancies that he understands them."

"Maybe he does," said Miles, "but that doesn't help me. I don't like this," he said, angrily. "I don't like it at all."

She said, after a moment, "I see. You couldn't, of course, feel otherwise." She added, "It's absurd to tell you this — but I'm lonely. Sometimes I find myself believing that if I had had a son — a son like you . . ."

He said, roughly, "Don't say it."

Helen smiled, a very little.

He came by appointment on the following evening, after dinner; Ole let him in and

Carol came out of the drawing room to meet him. She said, "I'm so sorry, Major Duncan, but Mother isn't here. She had to leave for Philadelphia this afternoon. She tried to get you on the telephone but you were out. I think she wired, however."

He said, "Gosh, I haven't been back at the hotel all day. I left this morning, ran into some fellows I knew, and a bunch of RAF men and we batted around together — we had dinner, finally, six of us . . ." He looked at her, his eyes bright. It had been a good day, full of good, hard talk. Dinner was good, too, and the liquor which went with it. There had also been a fight. Not too much of a fight because there were too many of them on the right side, and the management had arrived anxiously rubbing its hands.

He said, "Maybe I look a little out of formation? We got in a brawl. It was beautiful."

"Sit down," said Carol, "if you haven't something better to do, I'll have Ole bring us a drink."

"I've had enough." He sat down. He said, grinning, "I punched a guy in the nose. He sat at the next table. He had plenty of stomach and not much hair. He said, 'I don't care how long this war goes on, I'm making more than I ever made, it's jake with me.'"

Carol said, "I hope you killed him."

"No, worse luck," said Miles. "There's a hell of a lot of them, though. I've heard of it, but never ran into it before. S.O.B.'s like that," he said, "and guys that go on strike and the whole kit and biling of 'em." He laughed. He said, "And they ask us, what are we fighting for? We're too busy fighting to answer, maybe even to know. But if we're fighting for termites, I'm a conshie, from now on in. Or maybe I want to get back and just fight to *be* fighting, not caring much for what or who — is it," he inquired, "whom?"

"Skip the syntax," said Carol. She looked at him warily. He was keyed too high. It wasn't all the liquor.

He said, "Well, I suppose I'd better take off . . ."

Carol suggested on impulse, "Unless you'd rather not — won't you stay? We could scare up something."

"Where's the boy friend?"

"Washington."

He felt let down, flat as yesterday's beer. Helen wasn't here. He had come tearing to the house as fast as a startled taxi driver could bring him. He had been full of wise words, hot deeds and passable Scotch. He had come tearing up the steps to tell her, "I punched a guy in the nose for you, because you're

82

beautiful and desirable, because you know what it's all about." But she wasn't here, just this cool, gray-eyed girl who didn't especially like him.

Well, he could go out and find somebody or other and they could go on getting drunk or drunker, or he could go back to the hotel, read a good book and wish himself a thousand miles away . . .

Neither course appealed.

He said hesitantly, "Only if it won't bore you."

She said, "It's lateish. We might do a newsreel and then get something to eat."

They walked. It was warm, it was spring. The first two newsreel theaters were full to the doors. The third wasn't. They sat in the back row and girls and boys sat beside them, chewed gum, held hands, made love. The house was full of uniforms.

They laughed at Goofy, and at a Benchley short. They saw a clever propaganda short and Carol whispered, "That's Dudley's — he's been making them for a year." They saw a March of Time and then the battle films came on. She could feel him stir uneasily beside her. She was deeply sorry for him. Just a kid, and he's been from hell to breakfast.

Then, suddenly, he himself was on the

screen, speaking his few sentences, receiving his decoration.

"Let's get out of here," he said, in an agony of embarrassment.

But before they reached the street, people had recognized him, first an usher, perhaps, as they went up the aisle. People came out of the little house, flooded the lobby. Kids, wide-eyed. Soldiers. Soldiers' girls. They thrust programs at him and bitten pencil stubs. Would he sign, would he autograph this, would he autograph that?

Carol touched his arm. She said, "Better do it, Miles." And neither noticed that she had discarded a formality to which she had steadfastly clung.

They escaped finally, went uptown and across to the 59th Street Longchamps by taxi and found an obscured table. There weren't too many people there as yet. They ordered coffee, club sandwiches, and finally, ice cream. He couldn't, he told her, get enough ice cream.

He said, "You were swell to see me through."

"Thanks," she said, smiling, "not at all."

He focused his blue eyes upon her, as if he had never seen her before. In a sense, he had not, as he had never seen her without, somewhere nearby, her mother.

He said, "Lennox is a lucky guy."

"You really think so?"

"Sure," he said, "of course. You've got everything."

"Thanks," said Carol again. "I hope I have. It isn't easy being part of the Hillary legend."

Miles considered that soberly. He said, "No, I suppose not. I didn't think of that before. I don't suppose I ever really talked to you. Yet —"

She said, "Yet we keep running into each other on steps and in halls. How's the book coming?"

"Oh, that," he said, looking uneasy. "It's a lot of hooey, probably. If it's any good it won't be my doing." She was a swell girl and a pretty one. She was Helen's daughter. She was not the rose, the rose was in Philadelphia — but —

He said, "I suppose you think I'm nuts, but the book is mostly an excuse."

Carol nodded. She said, "I assumed as much."

"You did? Well, you know her better than I do," he said, "and how wonderful she is — how kind, and generous. Just being with her has meant a lot to me."

Carol said nothing. He nodded, wondering why he had said that, wishing he hadn't:

"Now you'll think I'm completely off the beam."

"No . . ."

Miles looked around restlessly. He asked, "Is there some place where we could go and dance? Not a night club."

She knew of such a place. They could have a drink there, she said. It was fair-sized, clean, not too crowded, and housed a mammoth jukebox. She told him about it. "Or would you rather we went to a hotel?" she asked.

He liked jukeboxes.

It was within walking distance. He took her hand and swung it idly. He said, "Wonderful night. I've thought of nights like this, too many times. Of cities and music and girls. You do, you know, when you never expect to see them again."

"I suppose so," said Carol. Her heart was playing tricks. She didn't like it. She didn't like discovering that, when Miles Duncan touched her, her heart knew it. He had never touched her before except to shake hands, and the time she had danced with him at Jenny's party.

They reached the place and ordered. Miles looked at her, and said, smiling, "Let's dance."

He stood up, tall and thin, took her into

his arms and they danced, in unity and in silence. He danced very well. So did Dudley Lennox and a hundred men she had known. But not like this.

She thought, angrily, It isn't possible.

It couldn't be. She was in love with another man, whom she admired and respected, to whom she responded. His kiss was exciting and his arms about her a refuge. Yet dancing with Miles Duncan was more exciting than any kiss she had ever experienced.

She thought, It's a crazy chemical attraction, an idiotic pull, and it doesn't mean a thing. Involuntarily she pulled herself away, sharply, and Miles asked, looking down, "Hey, what gives?"

He saw her eyes, stormy gray, dark with emotion, and against her sudden pallor, her mouth was violently crimson. He felt that the hand he held was very cold and asked quickly,

"What's wrong, Carol — don't you feel well?"

"I'm all right," she answered, with an enormous effort, "it's nothing. Let's go back to the table."

Nothing? A sudden insanity, a going-blind of the mind. Nothing — a stroke of lightning, an earthquake, a tidal wave. No more than these, no less disastrous.

Her knees shook, they reached the table after what seemed a century and she sat down abruptly. And Miles said, anxiously:

"You look all shot. Here, drink your high-ball."

Her hand closed around the glass and she saw with detachment that it was unsteady and the cool, smooth rim chattered against her teeth. She drank a little, her color returned, and she smiled, dimly.

"Don't look so concerned," she said, "Good heavens, I think I blacked out, just for a second."

He said, "I'll get the check and take you home."

"No — please don't fuss," she said. "I'm fine now."

He regarded her in bewilderment.

"You don't look like the fainting kind," he said, "you look damned beautiful as well as quite healthy."

She said, "Well, I'm healthy, at any rate. I put in some strenuous hours at the hospital where I'm a nurses' aide, last night. Maybe it was that —"

He said, "Finish your drink and we'll go."

"How about one more dance?" she suggested, and felt herself shaking again, inside.

Why not? Just to make sure.

They danced, presently, and it was the

same, and worse. Yet, when she had adjusted herself to it, when she grew more accustomed — if you ever become accustomed — it was very wonderful.

Dudley's ring was bright on her hand, and she did not know nor care.

She thought with a lunatic dazzling clarity, *Well, this is it. . . .*

Chapter Seven

It was Miles who finally suggested that they go home. He said, restlessly, "Let's duck out, shall we?" and Carol saw with her sharper perception that he looked tired and a little bored. She rose and agreed, "All right, let's go."

They walked a block or so looking for a taxi. At a corner, Miles stopped to buy the first edition of a morning paper. He looked at the headlines, standing under the dim street lights. War abroad and war at home. The paper was headlining strikes. He swore, not casually and aloud, and stepped to the curb to beckon a cruising cab. The driver stopped with a loud squawk of brakes and they got in. Carol asked:

"Why the picturesque profanity?"

"Sorry," he said mechanically, "only I'm getting to the place where I wish I hadn't come home. Sure, news reached us after a fashion, but you have to be back here, in the middle of the complacency and the pocket-picking, the politics and the commercial patriotism to realize what's going on. It makes me sick to my stomach."

"I know," she said, softly.

"No," he denied, "you don't. Damned few people know — nor care. Except the guys who are fighting this war in order to get it over. It's a tough proposition; we know that and sweat it out. But you can't expect us to enjoy it. A fight's one thing but a fight plus an obstacle race is another. And all the obstacles our fellow citizens put in our way are so many booby traps. I should be patting myself on the back. I'm alive. I'm walking around with ribbons on my chest. I can drink good liquor and sleep in a soft bed. I can dance with a pretty girl. A hell of a lot of good guys aren't drinking nor sleeping nor dancing. A hell of a lot won't, ever again. So what? So I'll hang around here a while, heroic as all get out, and then I'll go somewhere and instruct, and after that it's combat again —"

"Do you want combat again?" she interrupted and her heart closed like a fist.

He looked down at her. She could not see his expression very well but she heard him laugh, abruptly.

"My dear girl," he said, "don't be juvenile. Few who have experienced it and come out alive have any yen to return. We're not half-witted. We're not noble. We're scared stupid most of the time. No, I don't want it, Carol, but if they'll give it to me I'll take it and say thanks. Because I'd like to be in on the kill. Probably, I won't be."

"Why?" she asked, her voice low.

"Oh," he said impatiently, "you can try your luck too far. And there's no future in that."

"Which is," she said vigorously, "a purely negative attitude."

"Oh, sure," he said tolerantly, as one speaks to an importunate child.

Carol was silent. Then she asked, "What do you intend to do when you come back, for good?"

"If I come back," he amended. "I don't know — I wanted to be an architect once. I didn't get very far with it."

"If you come back?" she repeated. "I didn't say 'if', I said 'when.' "

"You're an optimistic little cuss," he said casually, "but we get out of the habit of talking about the if and when — even the guys who are married, who have wives and kids. Now and then, we sit around and make plans, just for the hell of it. Very few believe in 'em, it's just talking to hear ourselves talk. The future — if we have any — can take care of itself. The job is immediate, it's now."

The cab stopped and Miles got out. He

paid the driver and walked up the steps with Carol. He said, "It's been fun, thanks a lot." He hesitated. "I suppose Helen will let me know when she gets back?"

"I dare say she'll call you," said Carol, feeling extraordinarily tired. "She's supposed to be in before lunch."

"Tell her," he said, grinning, "I'm at her service — memoirs of a moron."

He gave her a sketchy half salute, as she put her key in the door and it swung open. " 'Night," he said, and turned away. But he stopped, and swung back. He asked, "Sure you feel all right?"

"Swell," she said, and was close to tears.

She felt all right, she felt just dandy. She was walking up the familiar stairs, her heart had wings and her feet were rooted in cement. She was in love with a man who hardly knew she existed, who expected to die one of these days and didn't care much; who was, if he were in love with anyone, in love with her mother. And she herself was engaged to be married to a man with whom she had thought herself in love — a lot she'd known about it — and with whom she should be in love, a man who loved her and who would encase her in security as in cellophane.

She thought, I'm all mixed up. It doesn't mean a thing. I went off the beam tonight, tomorrow I'll be back on it again.

She went to her room, and to bed. She thought resolutely of Dudley Lennox. She thought of his smile, of the way his voice sounded, of his dark face and intent eyes and stubborn chin; she thought of his arms around her and his mouth upon her mouth. She found she had lost the trick of remembering. She felt nothing, neither revulsion nor pleasure, not even indifference.

Then, quite against her volition, she remembered Miles Duncan's arms and her awareness of his nearness, and she began to shiver, her face was hot and her hands were cold, she was dizzy, lying perfectly flat in her bed, and her pulses were drumbeats.

Miles had not kissed her, nor was he conscious of her; yet she could feel this way about him.

It doesn't make sense, she told herself angrily, and with heartbreak.

In the morning she woke and for that split second between the dream and the waking, she was herself again, a girl with a job, a girl with an engagement ring. Then she remembered and was both ashamed and angry. She dressed, slowly, dreading to face Aunt Agatha's sharp eyes across the breakfast table, hoping that her father would not come down. Often he did not, but made early coffee in his study, drank it, alone, and then went to work without seeing a member of his household.

Just her luck, of course, to find him already at the table, shaven and scrubbed, his thick hair battered into seemliness, and scowling over a newspaper, exchanging comments with Agatha, stately at the table's head, behind the silver coffee urn.

"Hi," said Adam and "Good morning, Carol," said Agatha.

She smiled at them, managing a suitable greeting, looked with indifference at her orange juice, and with revulsion at the scrambled eggs Ole offered her. She said, "Just black coffee and some dry toast, please, Ole."

Adam raised a heavy eyebrow. One of the minor charms of his child was the fact that she did not diet, that her appetite was as healthy as a good child's, and her metabolism took care of her indulgence. Helen was "careful" because although she was tiny and slim, she was over forty. Helen went in for temperance, massage, fresh air, exercise and moderation.

"And where were you last night?" he inquired.

She said, "Miles Duncan came — he had a date with Mother to work on the book and she hadn't been able to reach him and cancel it, so he turned up, we went to a newsreel, and then to a couple of other places."

"I heard you come in," said Agatha. She stated, with reproach, "It was rather late."

"I'm a big girl now," Carol reminded her.

"Where," asked her father, "is your young tycoon?"

"In Washington," said Carol. "Do you think he'd like to hear himself called a tycoon?"

"Very much," said Adam promptly.

Carol rose. She had drunk her coffee, and part of her orange juice. An uninteresting looking piece of toast was carefully crumbled on her plate.

She said, "Back to the salt mines. Goodbye, darlings."

When she had gone Agatha looked at Adam. She asked:

"What's the matter with her?"

"Nothing, I hope," he answered, "but I passed up the sixty-four dollar questions, when they pertained to women, many years ago."

Agatha said, "I don't like the way she looks."

"I do," said Adam, "she looks like me."

"Don't be willful," she said, absently. "I mean —"

"You mean," interrupted Adam, "that, being young, Carol is fairly transparent. Or is she? She came in to breakfast, looking a trifle pale, and somewhat heavy around the eyes. She wouldn't eat. Which probably means, in modern diagnosis that she has a slight hangover. Young Duncan," he added, with respect, "has quite a capacity. Maybe she tried to keep up with him."

"I doubt it," said Agatha with asperity, "and trust not."

"Check," said Adam. "I have never seen my daughter plastered and I hope I never shall. So perhaps we may assume that she wasn't — last night."

"Naturally," said Agatha. "Personally, I think she's coming down with something."

Adam asked carelessly, "You don't think she's coming down with love?"

Agatha jumped. She said, "She's already in love."

"Oh," said Adam, and shrugged, "with Lennox. I'm not so sure."

"Why?"

He said, "If I were Carol I wouldn't be."

"My dear boy, you aren't Carol," Agatha reminded him.

Adam laughed. "Did you notice she wasn't

wearing the Lennox headlight this morning?"
he inquired.

"I didn't," said Agatha, "but what does
that signify? She may have decided not to
wear it to the office."

"Perhaps," said Adam, and lit a cigarette.
"Maybe she's found a new and more exciting
interest."

Agatha said bluntly, "You mean Major
Duncan. Don't be ridiculous."

He asked mildly, "What's ridiculous about
it? There's a powerful pull to a returned hero,
Agatha, and Duncan has the added appeal
of youth."

"Carol," said Agatha, "has always been
mature for her age and Dudley Lennox isn't
exactly senile. Besides —"

She hesitated and he asked, "Besides
what?"

"Nothing," said Agatha.

Adam put his cigarette in an ash tray.
"Come," he said, smiling, "it's not like you
to retreat. You were about to say, besides,
Major Duncan has eyes for Helen only."

Agatha flushed. She said, "That's not in
very good taste."

"Why not?" he said mildly. "We may as
well be sensible about it. You haven't lived
with us for as many years as Carol's been
alive not to know our situation. Personally,

I don't give a damn, as you also know. I've long relinquished hope that Helen would ever become a reasonable human being."

Agatha looked at him across the silver and crystal and flowers. The sunlight was warm in the big room, and her canary sang from its cage at the windows. She heard Ole clattering around the pantry. She said:

"I don't take sides. I never have. I couldn't, and make my home with you. But Helen acted in Carol's interest, Adam."

"Sometimes I wonder," he said. He added, "And I wonder too how much good it has done Carol, this publicly united family front. It's too late to speculate now," he said, "so we won't. But as far as I am concerned, if Carol wants Lennox, all right. If she has decided that she doesn't, okay too. She won't ask my advice so I won't give it. She won't ask Helen's, but Helen will give it anyway. Neither of us has earned the right to bestow it gratuitously, Agatha. If Carol consults anyone at any time, it will be you. Yet I doubt even that. She's a pretty integrated person for a girl of her age. I suppose she's had to be." He pushed back his chair and rose. "Don't worry too much," he suggested.

He went upstairs to his study. It was a rather bare, utilitarian workroom. Books were crowded on the shelves, and some were on the floor. There were a few pictures, several of Carol, one of Jenny Davis, one of a man who had been Adam Hillary's best friend and who had died in France in another war, and one of the plane he himself had flown.

He walked around the room restlessly. He thought, Well, if it's true all hell's loose.

He had been highly and authentically amused by his beautiful wife, flying in from further exploits with her tow-colored scalp at her small wrist. Fun and games. He'd been sorry for the kid, but he'd understood, more or less, his inevitable enchantment. He'd get over it, and go back where he belonged, sooner or later.

Perhaps his novelist's imagination was clouding his normal perception, he thought. Just because Carol turned up at breakfast with, obviously, a distaste for food, and ringless, that was no pattern for a plot. But if something had happened last night, if she had discovered an interest in Duncan, well, God help her, he thought; and, determined, if He won't, I shall!

Not that Carol had a chance against Helen. Or had she? he wondered. There was a lot on her side, youth, for one thing, virginity for another, and for the rest, those qualities which even a bedazzled kid might find miraculous, honesty, integrity, decency.

Which we haven't, he told himself somberly. Carol's a throwback. Helen isn't worth the powder to blow her up — and as for me. . . .

He went to a battered little cupboard, took out a bottle of Bourbon and poured himself a short drink. As a rule he did not drink before noon, or hadn't, for many years. He drank, and felt the oily smoothness warm and suave in his stomach. He looked at his desk and shook his head. He looked at the clock. Perdon would patter in presently. It lacked three minutes to the usual time of her arrival.

Three minutes passed. He occupied them contemplating the fact that if Carol had fallen in love with Miles Duncan, he, her father, was no longer amused. Perdon rapped and came in. Adam looked at her and smiled. He said, "My punctual Perdon," and she flushed as if he had embraced her. He waved his hand at the table. "Genius," he reported, "does not burn. I'm going out. There's a batch of script to be typed. I've left it on the desk —"

She asked docilely, "Where may I reach you?"

"I'll call in," said Adam vaguely, and went out.

Perdon looked at the bar glass, still wet. She picked it up, carried it into the bathroom, and washed it. She was disturbed. Mr. Hillary never drank in the morning to her knowledge. And right after breakfast, too. She shuddered. And also, she knew where he was going. When he was vague, when he promised to call in, he was going to That Woman.

Not that Perdon liked Helen Hillary. She disliked her very much. But you could hardly expect her to love Miss Davis. In the romantic type of book which Perdon read, curled up in her narrow bed in her respectable plush and gilt hotel, it was always to the faithful secretary that the great man turned when his married life was not all it should be.

Chapter Eight

Carol went to the office. There was plenty to do. She was busy all morning. Her head ached slightly, which annoyed her, so she worked until she had something to complain about. At lunchtime she went downstairs into the vast mazes of the building, sat at a restaurant table with three or four of her co-workers, and choked down a glass of milk. And one of them cried, "What's wrong, Carol, you look ghastly."

Carol said, "I feel it." She added glumly, "Got an aspirin?"

Three friendly hands offered three white tablets. She took them all.

One of the girls inquired, "What happened to your ring?"

Carol regarded her naked finger. She replied, with great simplicity, "I didn't wear it."

They shouted at her and she grinned and lit a cigarette. That had been a silly performance this morning. Put and take. Put Dudley's ring on and take it off. Perfectly idiotic. But it had seemed as heavy as a manacle, and just as desirable.

She said, "Stop cackling. I have the grand-mother of all headaches."

When she returned home her head still ached and she found her only consolation in the fact that it wasn't her night at the hospital, and that Dudley wouldn't be back from Washington. She had spent the day doing her job with competence, if not brilliance, and with the surface of her mind. Beneath that surface she was supremely preoccupied. She thought, So now what do I do, go into conference with Dudley, return his ring, say it was all a mistake, in the best tradition?

If she did, what happened after that? After that, she would be a young woman who had broken an engagement of short duration and was once again in the market. Only she wasn't in the market, she needn't shop around. She knew what she wanted. And what she wanted had a sold sign on it.

Maybe it would be smart to hang on to what she already had until —

Until when?

Besides, she no longer wanted what she had, which was very peculiar, as until last night she had wanted it very much.

Perhaps she ought to go on the air. Perhaps she should start right in practicing the opening gambit . . . *"my problem, Mr. Anthony —"*

Ole opened the door for her, cracked his wooden features into a grin and told her the daily news. Her mother was home, likewise her father and Major Duncan was expected for dinner.

Magically, Carol's headache was gone and she bestowed a dazzling smile upon Ole and fled upstairs. When she reached Helen's landing, Helen called her.

"Is that you, Carol?"

"In the flesh," said Carol. She felt perfectly wonderful. She went into the bedroom. Helen was in bed. She was sitting up, her spectacular hair tied back with a pale pink ribbon. She wore a wisp of rosy chiffon. She said:

"Come in, lamb. Philadelphia was terrific. I fought, tooth and nail — but I now have a contract. Of course, Jock fought too."

Jock was Hanson, her agent. Carol asked: "How many articles?"

"Six," said Helen. She added, "I got back, and went straight to bed, had lunch on a tray, a nap and then Cresson massaged me." She looked animated and lovely. "Miles is coming for dinner," she said, "and we'll work on the book afterward.

"How jolly," said Carol. She could feel

the little men returning, little men with spurs on their heels and hammers in their hands, tramping gaily through her head.

Helen looked at her. She asked, "Just what do you mean by that? I don't like your tone."

"I'm sorry," said Carol and shut the door after her. Helen regarded its blank whiteness, and felt herself frowning. With an effort she smoothed her face out, as with a mental iron. She thought, What's come over her?

Carol went upstairs. She ran a tub, undressed and dunked herself in the hot scented water and lying back, regarded her straight little toes. The obligato of hammers in her head ceased temporarily and her eyes felt as if she could open them wide without screaming. The tension in the back of her neck lessened and she turned her head cautiously and found that it could move and not break.

Nerves. A very bad case of the jitters because she had gone dancing last night and encountered the first shockingly relentless physical attraction of her life.

She sat up in the tub and the suds swished around her with a little boiling sound. "But I don't *want* that," she said, aloud.

It didn't last, everyone said so. She had had a shining example of that truth before her eyes for twenty-three years. What else had brought an iconoclastic instructor of English and a precocious youngster with red-gold hair together? What else could have culminated in a marriage less than a month afterwards?

She picked up the brush and the soap mitt and went to work. She'd dismiss this whole crazy business from her mind, she'd put her ring back where it belonged, and she'd run like the devil every time she saw Miles Duncan. He wouldn't be here forever. He'd get his orders once his leave was over, he'd go, heaven knew where, and she'd never see him again.

Which was all right with her; so the slow, hopeless tears slid over her wet, soapy face and she rubbed her eyes with a face cloth and then there were more tears, because of the soap.

Carol was a little late for dinner, and found Miles and Helen, Agatha and Adam finishing their drinks in the living room. Miles' and Adam's were dry martinis, Helen's was tomato juice, Agatha's, sherry.

Helen looked up as Carol came in. She said, pleasantly, "We had almost given you up — Ole has announced dinner. What do you want to drink?"

"Martini," said Carol, "and I'm sorry I'm

late — I'll take my cocktail to the table."

"Barbaric custom," said Adam, and poured her drink. "Consume it here in peace and quiet. Dinner can wait."

Miles asked, "Not speaking to me this evening?"

She had scarcely looked at him. Now she did. He had risen at her entrance, and was still standing, by the fireplace, his glass in his hand. She said, "Sorry, Miles — how apologetic I am all of a sudden! But you're just like one of the family now."

There was a distinct sting in her light voice. Miles' brows drew together and Adam looked quickly at Helen. But Helen was regarding Carol with astonishment. She said:

"Darling, do these old eyes fail me, or are those my earrings?"

Carol's hand went up to one ear. She said, and indicated her jade pendant, "They are indeed. I had to chloroform Cresson to get them but I thought — as long as I was wearing my jade.

Helen's earrings had been presented to her in China by a very distinguished gentleman. He was traveling at the same time and they were together part of the way; before she met Miles, the senator had procured the earrings from an equally distinguished ally and they were to be brought

108

home as a peace offering for his wife, who did not care much for his world tour, nor his political ambitions, but longed instead for the peace of her New England farm.

Now the earrings glowed with the special radiance of gem jade in Carol's ears, and her skin looked very white, her mouth very red; and there was green in her gray eyes.

"And," added her mother, "aren't you doing your hair a new way?"

Usually, Carol wore her curly hair brushed back from a casual part and curling behind her ears. Tonight it was swept up and confined by a curved, engraved gold band, a half circle, the ends fastened to narrow black velvet ribbons, which her hair concealed. It was a hair ornament of another generation which Agatha had given her years ago.

The hair-do gave her height and piquancy. She said, "I felt very Alice in Wonderland. But Miles must be bored with all this —"

"I'm fascinated," he said promptly. He smiled at Helen, and then looked at Carol, as she sat beside her father and lifted the glass to her lips. "Are you quite all right again?" he asked.

"Again?" repeated Helen, "what was wrong with her and when?"

"Last night," said Miles, before Carol could speak and she could have strangled him in hot blood, "we went dancing, and she had a spell of sorts."

"Spell?" said Adam. He thought, watching Carol's eyes, Maybe that's the word for it. . . .

Helen looked startled. She said, "Carol doesn't have spells!"

"You wouldn't know," said Carol composedly, "I have them all the time. I think they used to be called the vapors."

Agatha said, "Be serious. Was it something you ate?"

Carol laughed. "I haven't the remotest idea what I ate," she answered.

Ole appeared, looking plaintive. Helen rose. She wore a short black frock, beautifully fitted. What had possessed Carol to wear a long dress, and how effective the jade was with the paler green. Almost too effective, thought Helen crossly.

But she put her arm through her daughter's and looked up at her. She had to look up, a little. Having known for years that high heels and high hair are mere camouflage for a tiny woman, she capitalized upon her lack of inches. She never wore anything higher than cuban heels on the street, her evening slippers were made for her, and in the house she wore pumps the size and last of a dancing school child's or ballet slippers.

She asked, "Are you going out tonight? I thought Dudley was in Washington."

Carol looked at her ring as if it were a receiving set. She said, "He is. But I thought I might scare up somebody, over thirty-eight or 4F."

"Would I do?" inquired her father as they entered the dining room. "I answer the requirements and it's been a long time since we've had a binge together." He waited until they were seated. "How about it?" he asked his wife, "couldn't you and Miles forego the pangs of biography and step out with us?"

Miles looked interested but Helen said quickly, "No, it isn't possible. We have to work. My time is so limited and Miles may be off any day." She glanced at him just in time to see his face alter. "Why, Miles," she said, "would you like to go?"

He smiled at her. "No, of course not," he said, "but —" he shrugged, "I don't suppose I feel comfortable with the book yet," he confessed.

Adam said cheerfully, "Tell you what. We'll pick a spot, not too hot nor too bright, but bright and hot enough, and Carol and I will go there presently and when you two slaves are through with the evening grind, you can join us and we'll buy you a drink."

Helen looked, for her, uncertain, but Miles

said, "That would be swell, sir."

Adam said, irritably, "And forget the 'sir'. I can feel the beard grow in the grave." He looked at Agatha. "How about you?" he inquired. "It would do you good to get drunk, Agatha, once every ten years."

She said, calmly, "When my sister married Helen's father I had too much champagne." Her eyes twinkled. "She was younger than I," she told Miles, "and I was very fond of her and also a little in love with *him*. Anyway I was humiliatingly ill thereafter, so since then I have been abstemious. Besides," she added, "I have secured three excellent new records and four mysteries. I'll stay home, thank you just the same, Adam."

Helen said, "Now the family skeletons appear." She turned to Miles. "I think Aunt Agatha remained in love with my father," she said, "because when after Mother's death he remarried — I was about five at the time — she appeared like an avenging angel and swept me off to live with her. Poor father — not," she added thoughtfully, "that he cared."

"Nonsense," said Agatha, "and don't shock Major Duncan. Your father had the world's worst disposition, Helen. I learned that shortly after my sister married him. So, fell out of love."

Adam said, lightly, "Isn't it remarkable how soon you know you've fallen out, and how uncertain you can be that you've fallen in?"

After dinner, Adam changed . . . "I know it's wartime," he told Carol, "but I simply cannot be seen with you in all your glory, in hairy tweeds," called a taxi and he and Carol went out into the lovely night. He had sent Ole to the telephone during dinner, and as a result there would be tickets at a box office. How he managed these things no one knew. The tickets were for a musical which was a rival to Jenny's success. They missed most of the first act, of course, but the second was lively enough. Adam said, when they left the theater, having been stopped by a dozen people, "It's not far, shall we walk?"

She said, "What's the place like? New?"

"It's small and rather nice. A pretty girl sings, there's room to dance. I discovered it a couple of years ago. It isn't one of the more publicized *boites*. As I recall our final arrangements, we were to 'phone your mother and see if she and Miles were still working." He added, "I called Jenny at the theater before we left — she may join us later, if she can get away from a supper party . . ."

Well, that's cosy, thought Carol. She was fond of Jenny. She liked being with her. She

113

believed that she was very civilized about the situation, but nevertheless it made her uneasy.

They walked uptown a few blocks and presently turned, and there was the place, small, canopied, with a doorman who all but fell on Adam's neck. He had 'phoned for a table apparently. There it was in the corner, and a thin Frenchman was greeting Adam, in his own language. Adam presented him to Carol. He said, "Carol, this is Henri De —"

"Merely Henri," said the Frenchman.

"Henri," Adam corrected himself, "and this, Henri, is my daughter."

Henri said he was enchanted. He said, "She resembles you, a little." He added, "There will be others in your party?"

"Three, I think."

"I may order?"

"Of course."

When Henri had gone Carol said, "I'll find the little girls' room and do over my face. Who is Henri?"

"An old friend. I knew him in France."

Carol recalled that Henri walked with a limp. Adam went on, "I was billeted at his mother's house for a time. It was a lovely place, there were walled gardens and a silent, green park . . ."

She asked, "And he's here, doing this?"

"He's here. He's doing this," agreed Adam, "but perhaps other things besides. We won't talk of that. I'll 'phone your mother, while you're gone."

Carol went into the little powder room, spoke pleasantly to the maid. She thought, I bet a nickel father financed this place. She puzzled over that for a minute, and then she thought, I wonder if he'll come.

She was not thinking of Adam nor his old friend, Henri.

When she returned Adam was drinking Scotch. He rose and looked at her. He commented, "No visible improvement, as none was possible. My good friend Henri could kill me for drinking now. He has a special supper for us. And your mother and her little hero are joining us."

Carol said, "I wish you wouldn't call him that."

"Isn't he?"

"I don't know."

Adam offered her his cigarette case. She took a cigarette from it. It was very thin, satin smooth platinum. Jenny had given it to him, she supposed.

He said, "Carol, before they come, I want to ask you something."

"Yes?" Her voice was steady but her heart was not. His tone was very grave.

115

"Are you in love with Dudley Lennox?"

She said, quickly, "Of course," looked up, looked away. And added, honestly, "I thought so."

"And you don't think so now?"

"I'm not sure."

"Why?"

The probe hurt, she was restive under it. She asked, evasively, "How do I know? How does anyone know?"

"You've got something there," he agreed, "for certainly, if you aren't sure, then you can be sure you're not in love and likewise, if you are sure, it may not last forever."

She asked, after a moment, "Are some things worth wanting and trying to take even if they won't last?"

"I've always been of that opinion," he said, "which is damned silly of me."

Carol looked at the end of her cigarette. She said, "You write a lot about love. How much do you know?"

"Oh, nothing," he said, after a moment, "or everything. I've loved two women in my life — and I am not speaking of paternal affection, Carol. They were as different as possible, so perhaps I know a good deal after all."

"I'm sorry," she said, "I didn't mean — I shouldn't have asked that."

"No," he agreed, sadly, "intimacies between father and daughter, especially between a father and daughter who have lived together for twenty-three years on the hearty live-and-let-live plan aren't indicated perhaps."

She said, "let me ask you this, then. If you *know* an attraction is just physical — what do you do about it?"

Steady, he warned himself, here we have it, and it's no sixty-four dollar question as I have said to Agatha. It's worth a million dollars and unanswerable.

He said carefully, "Look, Carol, there has to be that or it's no good at all, see? No one, living or dead, can tell you how long it will last. It might last a week, a month, a year, ten years, a lifetime. It has, you know. That's something you find out for yourself, my dear. And while you're finding it out, you also discover if it's 'just', as you put it. It might not be *just* — it might be a great deal more. Only you have to grow into the other, the companionship and sharing and understanding. Hell, I'm talking like a novelist now. But it's true, novelist or not. If you grow into that, and the original pull remains, well, you're damned lucky. Not everyone has it all —"

She said, thoughtfully, "So if I have the

attraction to start with, then, it's worth a gamble?"

He looked up, as if compelled, toward the door. He said, quietly, "Here come your mother and Miles. As for its being worth a gamble, that's something you must decide for yourself."

He was tense suddenly, with excitement. He thought, She'll decide and I'll be around. I'm dealing myself in. I'll play it close to my chest, the smart way.

Watching Helen come toward them, noting that she too had changed — she had kept the kid cooling his heels and heart while she had done so — noting that she was as animated and lovely as he had ever seen her, his heart tightened. He didn't give a hoot about Mrs. Adam Hillary. But he gave considerably more than that for Mrs. Hillary's daughter. And he liked Miles.

He rose and smiled at them. He said, "You're just in time."

Chapter Nine

They reached the table and Helen looked inquiringly at the fifth chair. Adam explained. "Jenny may drop in."

Helen said, "That's nice," and regarded the small room with composure. She commented, "But this is a very attractive place."

They sat down, and Miles ruffled his eyebrows into a half scowl as Carol asked, brightly, "How did the work go?"

"Not so hot," he told her, and Helen sighed. She said, smiling:

"I can't do anything with him. He gets going beautifully, and then clams suddenly when I ask questions."

"Perhaps you ask the wrong ones," suggested her husband pleasantly.

Henri appeared and Adam said, "I don't think we'll wait for Miss Davis, Henri." He presented the thin dark man to Helen and Miles. Henri's face regarding Helen was flattery itself, but it also seemed rather bewildered. He shook the hand Miles offered and said, "This is a privilege, Major."

Adam said, carelessly, "When Miss Davis comes no doubt she will want her usual . . ."

Henri's face went blank with amazement, but he managed to say, "Of course, Adam."

When he had gone Helen said, lightly, "Poor little man. He was trying so hard to be discreet!"

Adam said, flatly, "Jenny and I have come here often since the place opened. We like it."

"You seem to know him rather well," Helen said.

"In France," Adam told her. "I told you about it — you've probably forgotten."

Her eyes opened wide. She said, "Not Henri Marie De—"

"Just Henri," he interrupted, "which is the way he prefers it." He explained to Miles, "As I told Carol, before you joined us, I was billeted at his mother's place. We were good friends. He has been in this country since just after the fall of France. How he got here we do not inquire, nor do we examine his present activities — those which have very little to do with the restaurant business. Inquiries would render them useless."

Miles said with respect, "I get it," and Helen said crossly, "If he's connected in some way with the underground, why not say so and let it go at that? You're so devious, Adam." She thought a moment, and then added, "He had, I believe, a sister?"

"He had," said Adam briefly, "but she died."

"I begin to remember," said Helen.

Carol was hot with embarrassment. What must Miles think? She had often been present at various verbal skirmishes between her parents. She hadn't enjoyed them but they weren't her business. Now, suddenly, they were. She glanced at Miles and found him staring at Adam with hostility. She said quickly, "Let's dance, Miles."

The little orchestra was playing a waltz. The atmosphere of the whole place was three-quarter time, muted, gentle, unhurried. Miles rose and Carol went into his arms. She saw her mother regarding her with speculation and the blood rose hot to her cheeks.

Adam watched them dance. He addressed his wife, amiably. He asked, "They look well together, don't they?"

"Why yes," said Helen easily, "very well."

"So well," Adam remarked negligently, "that I'd like to promote a — an understanding between them. Miles would make a congenial son-in-law provided he'd get over his natural dislike for me."

Helen said, shortly, "That's ridiculous."

"At the moment, yes," agreed Adam.

Miles and Carol danced in silence. She

didn't want to talk, besides what was there to say? But she moved closer to him quite consciously and his reaction was automatic. He tightened his arm about her, bent his tall head and felt the silken touch of her hair against his cheek. He spoke for the first time, aware of a pleasurable excitement which astonished him. "No swooning on me to-night, mind," he warned her, laughing.

She said, with a sedateness she did not feel, "I'll try not to, Miles, but I promise nothing."

She lifted her head and he would have been both blind and stupid to ignore the soft, luminous regard, and the deliberate challenge of her red mouth. He demanded, "Hey, what are you trying to do?"

"If you don't know," said Carol, her heart hammering, "I've failed. I must be slipping."

"You don't look like a two-timing gal," said Miles. "What would Lennox say?"

Carol shrugged. "I wouldn't know," she admitted, "as the situation has not arisen before."

He said, as if astonished, "I don't believe I ever realized how pretty you are —"

Carol said, "It's high time." She looked toward their table, as they came closer to it and added with resignation, "Mother is sending up smoke signals."

They danced up to the table and stopped. And Helen said sweetly, "Soup's on."

Henri's supper, delicate and ineffable, was being served. It consisted of an omelette which was out of this world, a good Chablis, and salad, expertly tossed, merely breathed upon by the garlic. Coffee and sweet to follow, Adam told them.

"This is marvelous," said Miles with reverence, and almost reluctantly touched his fork to the yellow cloud. Helen looked from him to her daughter. She said, smiling, "You two seem to be getting on better."

"Haven't we always?" inquired Carol, but Miles cut in. He said, "Ah!" with satisfaction as the omelette melted in his mouth. Then he grinned at Helen. "You ought to keep her under lock and key," he suggested, "or at least until Lennox comes home. I believe, God knows why, that she's trying to make me."

"Just to keep my hand in," Carol assured him earnestly.

Good, thought Adam in rising excitement, she's serious, he doesn't know it and she's careful to see that he doesn't. But it puzzles him, and he likes it.

Helen said nothing, but her rosy mask concealed considerable irritation. She was glad when, a moment later, Jenny entered. She

123

came straight to their table, sank in the chair waiting for her and cried, "I thought I'd never get away." Her eyes, turned on Adam, were brilliant. "Hello everybody," she added, smiling. "I've just run out on two first-string critics and a beautiful young man."

Adam asked, "Have you had anything to eat?"

"One glass of champagne and a saltine."

Helen shuddered. She said, "Darling, what a combination!"

"The champagne was ages ago," said Jenny, "and one saltine does *not* stick to the ribs."

"Helen said, "Well, now you can eat in peace. Adam, do get a waiter. The service," she went on, "is remarkably good. Of course it's my first time here and you and Adam are probably *persona grata*."

Jenny's eyes fled to Adam's but his face was still and unrevealing. He said, "Henri has your supper order, Jenny."

Henri came, following the boy with the tray, and Miles, surveying Jenny's supper, laughed, greatly entertained. Crackers and milk, bread, butter, and brown sugar. Also, carrot sticks.

"Minerals," explained Jenny gravely, "protein, calcium, and a dash of vitamin A."

"How perfectly ghastly," Helen murmured. She had scarcely touched her omelette and salad and her wineglass was full.

"Our Jenny," said Adam, "has gone on a diet — after midnight. She now eschews the succulent lobster, the creamy chicken á la King, the guinea hen under glass."

The sound of crackling carrots was loud, as Jenny chonked effectively. She said, "I feel ever so much better — not that I ever felt badly."

Helen smiled, with an effort. She asked Miles, "Would you care to dance with an elderly female who detests carrots?"

He rose with alacrity but at that moment the lights went down, and the baby spot shone on the girl who had just appeared at the piano. So they sat down to listen to her. She was small and dark, with straight black hair hanging to her shoulders and with heavy bangs. She had the face of a wistful monkey and beautiful hands. She sang in French. Her songs were quiet and nostalgic her voice was small and lovely. Carol's heart constricted. All the sad, lovely, wonderful, hopeless things she had felt since the night before were here, in the dark velvet voice, smooth as cream, haunting as a remembered spring. It was not a night club voice. It was scented with fresh lilacs rather than Chanel Number Five.

A large, wet tear slid down her cheek and she swallowed, making a soft, forlorn sound, like a child. Miles, next to her, was the only one who heard. He put his hand out and touched her. "Hey," he whispered, "what's wrong?"

"Nothing," she said fiercely, "do be quiet!"

But the lights came on, and he was not the only one who saw her touch her handkerchief to her cheek in a swift, ashamed gesture.

Carol rose, before the encore, excused herself and went to the powder room. And Miles asked, "What happened, she was crying!"

"Carol never cries," said Jenny. Her little face was anxious and she looked at Adam, who shook his head at her slightly. He said, low, "I felt like crying too — it's a rather lovely song. It's all of a France which used to be but which has not existed for years except in sentimental imaginations."

Helen said sharply, "She can't feel well."

"Maybe she's in love," suggested Adam, carelessly.

"Of course she is," said Jenny, wide-eyed. "Do you suppose she and Dudley have quarreled?"

"I suppose," said Adam, "nothing of the kind. I'd quite forgotten the little gentleman with his finger on the nation's pulse."

"But," began Miles, and closed his mouth tight. He flushed, picked up his wineglass and drank, hastily. Adam watched him with satisfaction and Helen rose. She said in tones of the utmost concern, "I'd better go and see what's the matter."

She found Carol alone in the blue and rose room, sitting before the mirror, repairing her lipstick, doing things with a powder-filled bit of cotton. Helen sat down beside her, at the next mirror and took out her own weapons. She asked, "What in the world happened to you, Carol?"

"Nothing," said Carol, "can't a girl raise a hand and be excused? It happens every day."

Her mother said, "You were crying. We all saw it."

Carol said, "I liked the song."

"You sit through *Tristan* dry-eyed. I've seen you."

"I don't like Wagner."

Her mother said, coaxingly, "If there's anything wrong, tell me. Perhaps I can help you. Have you and Dudley quarreled?"

"How come you dreamed that up?" said Carol.

"It was Jenny's suggestion."

"She's wrong," said Carol, "we haven't — yet."

"Yet?"

Carol said, after a moment, "When he returns I'm breaking my engagement."

Helen's color vanished, with shock. She asked, incredulously. "Are you out of your mind?"

"No," said Carol, "not any longer. I've decided that I don't want to marry him. It's customary to break the engagement in such circumstances."

Her mother said, "But what *has* he done?"

"Nothing. And don't look at me so helplessly. You aren't, really," Carol said.

Helen rose and closed the silver-gilt frame of her brocade bag. She said, "Well, I must say I'm very sorry for Dudley. He is sincerely in love with you. He doesn't deserve this."

"No," agreed Carol, "probably not."

"You have never been fanciful before," said Helen.

Carol forced herself to look at her mother. She kept her eyes cool and her voice even. She thought, angrily, Why does she have to be so beautiful? She thought, heavily, I've never really loved her, I've never even been very fond of her, I've just been sort of exasperatedly crazy about her because she is so lovely and because she does all the things I'd like to do, and can't. . . .

She said, "You wouldn't know. Perhaps

I'm full of whimsies. You aren't around much, Mother."

Helen said quietly, "Are you reproaching me?"

"Why should I," Carol asked, "at this late date?"

Helen said, still quietly but with vigor, "Carol, you aren't a child. You have known for years how matters stand between me and your father. You are quite intelligent enough to realize that we have remained together — ostensibly, that is — for your sake. And that," she added, bringing up the heavy artillery, "was my idea, not his. He was most reluctant."

Carol said, after a moment, "Well?"

"Well what?" asked her mother. "I don't understand you at all. One moment you go to pieces because a girl sings a stupid little song, which she enunciated so badly that I fail to see how anyone could translate the words — and the next, you are utterly without feeling."

Carol said, "I don't think you've gained anything, Mother. I haven't had much of a life between you."

"I suppose," said Helen, "the next thing you'll say is that you didn't ask to be born!"

"It's cliché, certainly," Carol agreed, "but — *did* I?"

Helen said, quickly, "When I first knew that your father and I couldn't possibly be happy, when I realized that practically any woman meant more to him than I, I determined it need not wreck my life nor complicate yours. I determined I would be successful, for you, and for me. And I have been."

"You have been," amended Carol, "for yourself."

Her mother was silent. Then, she said, "You are behaving very badly and are extremely impertinent as well. Just one thing more — are you serious in saying you intend to break your engagement to Dudley Lennox?"

"Quite serious."

Helen asked, slowly, "Are you in love with anyone else?"

"Why, naturally," Carol answered. This was it, and she braced herself for it.

"May I ask, with whom?"

"You may ask," said Carol, and her smile was dazzling. She added a touch of unnecessary rouge to her bright lips and put a coin in the china plate on the dressing table as the maid appeared suddenly, very old and thin in her black frock and white apron.

Carol spoke to her in French and went to

the door. She said, cheerfully, "I'm ready, Mother, are you?"

"Quite," said Helen.

Carol's knees were paper but she ignored them and the fact that her hands were cold and she felt a little ill. It was all right. It was out in the open. They were both ready.

The maid looked after them. Mother and daughter; the older woman looking so young and so very beautiful, the younger one, well, perhaps not as beautiful, but youth is always lovely. And such friends, she thought, like sisters. It was all very sentimental and charming. She sighed, with pleasure, plucked the coin from the saucer and from force of habit rang it thoughtfully on the glass of the dresser. It was honest coin.

Chapter Ten

Carol was on her way to breakfast the next morning when Cresson popped out of Helen's room and beckoned her. She reported in a stage whisper, "Mrs. Hillary wishes to see you, Miss Carol. She has not had a good night and her head aches."

Carol went in. The room was darkened and Helen wore a black eyeshade. It lent her an air of masquerade. Her chiffon nightgown and matching jacket were daffodil yellow and her hair wore a yellow ribbon.

"Good morning," said Carol cheerfully, keeping her voice muted in deference to the prevailing atmosphere.

"What's good about it?" Helen asked.

"Everything," said Carol, "the sun's shining, it's hot, and in another week or so I think we can open the cottage."

The cottage was on Long Island, available for weekends for Carol, with a good local maid, and weekends for Adam and Helen and their guests, when they were home and amenable.

Helen shook her head. She said, "Cleaning and drapes, and wrestling with ration stamps! I think we won't bother this year. If Marta could go down it would be different but she won't, and besides, she has to be here."

"I'll wrestle," said Carol. "Cresson said you wanted to see me."

It was strange talking to a woman behind a mask. Or had she always worn it? Helen's mouth was composed. She said, "Yes. When do you expect Dudley back?"

"Tonight. He's coming here for dinner."

Her mother said, "I shall be out. I have to go to the Anzac Club — and I thought it might interest Miles to go with me. Afterward we'll work."

Carol said, "That will be nice."

"I have almost enough material," Helen said, "there are just a few more things —" her voice trailed off.

"It must be a very small book," said Carol courteously.

"They're usually small," said her mother, "Miles isn't a war correspondent," she added with some acidity, "and also it isn't the story of his life. It's the story of his flying, the various mission — these books are more effective if they are brief. *Metropolis* wishes to publish it, complete in one issue, before book publication," she added.

"That's fine," said Carol.

Helen said, "He doesn't want the money. It's to go to the National War Fund." She moved her shoulders under the yellow chiffon.

Carol asked patiently, "Was that what you wished to tell me?"

"I didn't wish to tell you anything." With a sudden, sharp gesture Helen snatched away the eyeshade. Her black eyes blinked once or twice, accommodating themselves to the dim light. She asked, "Were you serious when you said you intended to break your engagement?"

"You asked me that last night."

"I haven't slept much since," said Helen, "so I'm asking you again."

"The answer," said Carol, "is the same."

Her mother said, "You are being absurd." She hesitated, which was unusual. She added, "And I can't imagine . . . that is to say, to my knowledge you've met nobody since your engagement, except Miles Duncan."

"That's right," said Carol.

"But you can't *mean* that," said Helen, and sat up to stare at her daughter. "You can't. It must be somebody you knew before."

"There isn't," said Carol, and smiled.

Helen lay back against the pillows. She

said, after a moment, "Am I to understand that you are in love with Miles?"

"Can you?" asked Carol.

Helen said impatiently, "You're as devious as your father. Of course I can understand, academically. He's young, attractive, and a hero. An unbeatable combination. Dudley hasn't a thing but charm, good looks, success and most of the money in the world!" She added, "While Miles has the added interest of being poor, practically nothing but his pay, and absolutely no future. He will return to combat eventually, and if he comes home —"

"He'll come home."

Helen said, "You are utterly fantastic. What leads you to think he is interested in you?"

"Nothing."

Her mother persisted. She said, "Has he — *is* he interested in you?"

Carol went to the door. She opened it and turned and smiled with marvelous self-confidence which she in no way felt. "Not yet," she said, and closed the door, softly.

Helen rang for Cresson. She ordered, "Get me black coffee and aspirin." She waited till the woman had gone, then lay back against the pillows.

She said to herself, *I won't have it.*

It was not the first time. But on the prior occasion the odds had been against the Hillarys' daughter. Carol had been twelve years old, a long-legged, colty child, all eyes and undisciplined hair and she had suffered braces on her teeth during that year. The young man had been twenty-five and a painter. He had painted Helen's portrait, the one which now hung in the drawing room. He had been a fine artist and he understood women, a little too well. All women, that is, save Helen, which had made quite a situation. He had understood Carol and her funny little girl adoration. He had been both sweet and sensible about it. It had not embarrassed him in the least, but Helen, impatient with Carol, although it had amused her, had been sorry for him. So she took a firm hand and ended it. She had explained the facts of life to her child, and in intimate detail. Carol already had known these in a sketchy sort of way. But now she suffered the maternal routine of you're-getting-to-be-a-big-girl-now — and the explanation that Mr. Carmen might not like big girls flinging themselves at his neck, sitting on his lap and following him around the house like a puppy. It was however, normal, said Helen, with her modern approach and just another manifestation of growing up which adults called the beginning of adolescence. Normal, but silly. Carol should pay more attention to the nice little boys in dancing school.

But now Carol was no longer twelve and the facts of life had not been a shock to her for years.

Helen was nearly forty-five. Five more years to fifty and then a decade to sixty. Women, especially women of her type, kept their charm until seventy. But that charm began to wilt around the edges or, at least, to alter in quality, long before seventy was reached. At fifty she would still be extravagantly admired but not by boys of twenty-four. At least, not after the fashion in which Miles Duncan admired her.

It was a very warm day, but Helen shivered, experiencing a deep, inexplicable exhaustion — it was as if, for a very long time, she had been running a race, fleetly, easily, always keeping well ahead of her opponent. Then one day, the distance between them lessened, the margin of safety no longer existed, she became aware of fatigue, and panic overtook her.

That afternoon, at the office, Dudley telephoned Carol. He asked, "Darling . . . have you missed me?" and Carol said, startled,

"Dudley, where *are* you?"

"In Washington. But you haven't answered."

She asked, "Why in Washington? I thought you were on your way home by now."

He said, "That's why I'm 'phoning. I'm held up. I'll fly in tomorrow sometime. May I have a rain check on dinner?"

She said desolately, "I'm so sorry."

"That's more like it," he said, and could not realize that her unhappiness was because the inevitable must be postponed. All last night, all today, she had been bracing herself for it. Now it would be another twenty-four hours and more.

"Tell me," said Dudley, "what you've been doing."

"Nothing much," she answered, with an effort. "Father took me out last night to a funny little French place — Miles and mother joined us and later, Jenny."

He said ruefully, "Just my luck not to be there."

He went on talking. Washington was unbearably hot. People melted where they stood. An egg had fried a reporter on the Capitol steps, he said, absurdly. The air conditioning in his suite had gone wrong. He missed her very much. He loved her as

138

much as he missed her.

Once, he said, "You don't sound like yourself, Carol."

She said, with some desperation, "I have a headache, it's nothing . . ."

When he hung up she leaned back in her chair and contemplated the universe. There was nothing very good in it. There was only the obligation to be herself, and honest.

Miles likes me, she told herself firmly, I knew it last night. I could feel it. He was, even, a little attracted. She set her small, square jaw. She thought, I'll have to play it my way, with every trick I know, and some I can learn. It's my life — and it's worth, she thought, remembering her conversation with Adam, a gamble. It may not be honest in one way, but at least I'm honest with myself.

Before she was ready to leave the office she telephoned home to say that Mr. Lennox would not be dining that night and that she would get something now and go to the hospital. It was not her regular evening but they could use her, they were sinfully shorthanded. She asked Ole, hopefully, "Are there any messages for me?"

There were none, he said, and reported, in his routine fashion that now only Miss Stuart would be at home this evening.

Carol went out of the building and across the street to a restaurant she liked. She had a club sandwich and a pot of hot, strong tea and some good little cakes. She sat at a corner table and abstractedly watched the room fill up. She ate, paid her check and took a taxi to the big hospital uptown.

Her blue uniform was in her locker, she changed and presented herself on the floor and was greeted with delight. One of the aides whose night it was had telephoned that she was ill and could not come. Miss Hillary was, therefore, a godsend.

She worked until shortly after nine o'clock — she was always competent and quiet, the charge and floor nurses liked her. The interns liked her too and were open about it when an opportunity offered, which wasn't often. She was in the children's ward which she liked very much but which broke her heart. She did the things she had been trained to do, very well indeed, relieving the graduate and student nurses.

When she let herself in at the Hillary house she was tired. It was a good sort of fatigue, it made you feel useful. Perhaps she would sleep, and not lie awake thinking, trying to see her way clear, trying to figure out what had happened to her, to minimize or rationalize it. You simply couldn't rationalize fall-

140

ing in love. You could analyze and call upon your last ounce of common sense. But it did no good. It was like believing. Either you believed or you didn't.

As she entered the hall Adam came out of the drawing room to meet her. He asked, "Where in the world have you been?"

"Didn't Ole tell you? Dudley is tied up in Washington, so I had something to eat after work and went on to the hospital."

He said, "I had dinner with Hodge, he's in from Boston. We talked book." He grinned. "He talked, that is. It isn't going well and I wish I had the guts to scrap it and start over. Come on in," he suggested. "Agatha has gone upstairs to play Sibelius and read a thriller — I'm having a quiet and morose drink. Want one?"

"No, thanks," she said, but suddenly she did not want to go up and shut herself in with her thoughts. She went into the drawing room and sat down beneath Helen's portrait. The painted loveliness looked down on her with a faint smile.

She asked, with an effort, "Where's Mother?"

His face was bland. "Working with Miles, I understand. It appeared it was too distracting here with the Girls bobbing in and out —" Helen always referred to her brace of

141

secretaries as the Girls — "so she went to his hotel. They were to dine there."

He looked at her and was silent, waiting. After a moment Carol said:

"Let's walk over and rout them out. Miles could buy us a drink."

Adam grinned. Good girl, he thought, that's the ticket. Straight to the mark and no nonsense about it. He rose, "Okay," he said, "let's go."

She said, "Just a minute. I look like a hag."

There was a powder room under the stairs, spacious and well fitted. She tore in, flung off her hat — she hated hats anyway — and the jacket of her faille suit. She washed her face, took cream from a crystal jar, put hot towels against her cheeks and eyes. She dipped cotton in astringent and worked in a little foundation. She powdered, renewed her lipstick and combed her hair. Her eyes looked back at her, bright and clear, she saw her flushed cheeks and her mouth curving into a smile. She had erased all trace of fatigue. It wasn't hard, at her age.

She came out and joined Adam. She said gaily, "I'm ready."

"So I see," he responded gravely. He left word with Ole where they would be, and they went out and walked down the street, away from the river. Miles' hotel was nearby, a small, square, uncompromising structure, with a good common-sense lobby. The clerk spoke to Adam. He knew the Hillarys. They came in sometimes for a scratch meal or went to the pleasant bar. He liked to tell new guests, "The Hillarys live in the neighborhood."

Adam said, "Hello Perkins," and went to the house 'phone.

When he hung up he walked back to Carol. He said, "No answer."

She frowned slightly, and Adam spoke to the clerk. He asked, "Have you seen Mrs. Hillary and Major Duncan?"

The clerk had. He had seen them come in late in the afternoon, he said; Mrs. Hillary had stopped to speak to him, to ask for his little boy who had been ill. He hadn't seen them again and he'd been at the desk ever since. He'd come on at five — they'd lost the regular night clerk to the service and he was filling in for the time being, the assistant manager would relieve him, at midnight.

Adam wasn't listening. He said, "I think the 'phone's off the hook, so we'll go on up."

He took Carol's arm and they walked toward the elevator. She asked, after a moment, "Was it?"

"What?"

"Off the hook?"

143

He said, "That's the way it sounded to me."

They were silent until they reached Miles' floor. They got out and walked down the corridor, and stopped in front of the suite which he had occupied since his arrival in New York. Adam said, "This is exactly the reverse of the Marines have landed."

He put his hand on the doorknob, it turned, they walked into the small foyer and stopped at the living room archway to regard the spectacle of Helen Hillary crying bitterly in Miles Duncan's arms.

Chapter Eleven

Adam did not look at his daughter. He knew, without looking, that she was white as paper, as transparent as glass. He cleared his throat and demanded, with mild concern:

"What's going on — are you ill, Helen?"

Carol watched her father move forward, very lightly and quickly for so big a man. She could not have stirred had it meant her life. Her entire being was a battleground of emotions, anger, grief, humiliation — but she could not look away. She was forced to see Miles start, and turn a bright, uncompromising scarlet. She heard him stammer something. But her hearing seemed dulled, the blood beat in her ears. She saw her mother draw away from Miles, not too hurriedly, and scrub at her face childishly with a large handkerchief, which certainly wasn't hers.

Helen spoke, as clearly as she could. She said:

"I'm so sorry, everybody."

Miles was recovering. He said, "She's overtired, that's all — she wouldn't eat — she hardly touched dinner —"

Adam commented, "The intellectual life is an exciting one," and Helen flashed him a look of pure hatred. Miles' eyes focused on Adam and antagonism was bright in them. He said, shortly:

"I don't know anything about the intellectual life but I do know that Helen is worn out."

She said, her voice catching, "Carol, please don't stand there, staring at me. Help me pick up the pieces . . ."

Carol's feet moved forward involuntarily, and she took her mother's hand without looking at Miles. She asked, stonily, "Where are your things?"

"I left them in Miles' bedroom," Helen said.

When the women had left Adam said, with his habitual and deceptive mildness:

"Don't be too upset, Miles. Women, especially those who have reached Helen's age, are apt to fall apart at the seams now and then. You are quite right, of course, she drives herself and she is no longer able to take it. Not that she'd admit it."

Miles flushed again. Adam thought, That's something of a body blow. He doesn't want to think of her as "that" age — but from now on in, he will!

Miles said, "Well, Lord, I don't know what happened exactly, we'd had dinner up here, and after they took out the table, we went on working. The book, such as it is, is done. At least, my part of it — so we sat talking about it and I told her I'd had my orders this morning — I hadn't mentioned it before — I'm going to be at Mitchell for a while and then sent somewhere to instruct. I said, I guess that she had enough dope and that, anyway, if the book were any good it would be up to her. And pretty soon she began to cry. She got up and started to leave the room, but I stopped her —"

"You needn't explain," said Adam, kindly, "I don't misinterpret. I'm not that kind of a husband."

Miles looked sulky, his face grew dark. What he hadn't and couldn't explain was that what he and Helen had talked about hadn't been the book, but Helen, herself. She had done the talking; her misery, her unhappiness, the fact that she had remained with her husband because of Carol, "not that Carol cares — she has never cared for me, not since she was a baby. I was away a good deal, or working, I had to in order to support her, while Adam was tearing around the face of the globe — so she turned to Aunt Agatha. And when he came back, when we were together again — not that I've lived with him for years, Miles, I couldn't and keep my self-respect — it was her father she admired. He had everything, the glamour, the romance — and he spoiled her terribly."

Miles had said something, taking her hands, trying to comfort her, but she would not be consoled. She had cried out that it wasn't fair, that she hadn't wanted the success for herself, that she was lonely, desperately lonely. Nothing had compensated, she said. She had hoped that Carol would — but she had long since given up that idea. And now Miles was going away, and she had seen in him the son she had never had, the understanding companion . . .

Which was where her husband and her daughter had come in.

Adam said, "Forget it. Helen thinks of herself as a perennial twenty-five. She isn't, you know. She's twenty years older than that. I don't have to draw you a physiological picture, do I? There's nothing to do but be patient. I'm sorry we chanced in and embarrassed you. It was, by the way, Carol's suggestion. Her wonderful young man didn't come back from Washington, after all, so she put in a hard evening's work at the hospital —"

"Does she?" said Miles, "I didn't know. She didn't tell me."

"She doesn't talk about herself," said Adam. "Anyway, back she came on the tired side, found me, and suggested that we walk around here and dig the two of you out to have a drink somewhere."

Miles had been very glad of the change of subject. He had been violently sorry for Helen, and completely her champion. He had held her in his arms for the first time since their return and felt her tears and smoothed her hair with his big hand. Yet instead of experiencing the physical excitement and emotional elation he had expected, he had felt singularly awkward. It was a little too sudden and it hadn't been of his making. And that sentence — about the son she had never had — hell, that threw him off, and he found himself, quite without volition, feeling rather like a son. Which wasn't how he had expected to feel, if at any time and by miracle, he had found Helen Hillary in his arms. He had held her close during a very nasty air raid, a world away, and had been flattered, excited, protective — not that she was as scared as he had been. But, tonight —

Adam said reflectively, "I still think a drink's indicated."

Miles looked at him doubtfully. It was

hard to adjust the picture. He had never liked Adam; first, before knowing him, simply because he was Helen's husband, and, after meeting him, for the same reason. Yet during the occasions on which they had been together he had felt himself gradually being disarmed. He'd even read the guy's book and it was a honey. It said so many of the things you felt and couldn't say. And they'd talked together now and then. Adam Hillary understood many things, even at his age and at his distance from the present war. You would have sworn he was regular, and rugged. But, against that altering picture, Helen's story of brutality and neglect, of other women! Jenny Davis was a proof of that. Since knowing the Hillarys, Miles had heard about Jenny from one source or another.

He found himself thinking for the first time, How does Carol feel about that, how does she feel about everything?

Carol sat on the edge of Miles' bed, absently smoothed the pillow with her hand, and watched Helen. Helen had washed her face in the small bathroom, and was now sitting at the dressing table repairing the damage. She seldom cried and she didn't cry well. Few women do, after thirty. After twenty-five, perhaps. Tears are hard and they disfigure. She said, ruefully, "I look dreadful."

Carol was quiet. Her mother looked back at her. She ordered sharply, "Don't sit there, saying nothing!"

"What is there to say?"

"Oh, anything," said Helen recklessly, "that I'm a fool, that I'm having an affair with Miles, that you walked in on a scene!"

Carol said coolly, "I don't think you'd be that much of a fool."

"I'm not," said Helen, "I was tired, that's all. I've been torn to pieces since I got back. I'm sick of being places Tuesday at two and Thursday at six."

"Then why don't you stay home?" asked Carol reasonably.

Her mother said, "You are deliberately exasperating. I can't and you know it. And also you have upset me very much, with this ridiculous talk of breaking your engagement."

"Why?" asked Carol. "It's my engagement."

Helen flung down her little comb. She said, somewhat wildly, "And now Miles has his orders"

Carol was very still. Then she opened her handbag and took out a cigarette. She took the matches from the bedside table. She closed the bag again. She said, smoking, and steadying her voice:

"Where does he go?"

"First, Mitchell Field . . ." Helen halted. She said, "I'm very fond of him, it's like seeing my own son sent back into combat."

"Nuts," said Carol. "He isn't your son, you wouldn't want him to be. You never wanted a son, nor," she added, "a daughter, for that matter."

Helen swung around. "Are you trying to tell me I'm in love with the boy?" she demanded.

"No," said Carol and her heart was light, suddenly. "I know you're not. You're not in love with anyone and you never will be. You don't want to love, you want to be loved. And you have your own dignity. You would never want to be in love with a boy twenty years your junior and don't want anything from him but a sort of hopeless adoration. This has happened before, Mother, and it will happen again — perhaps."

Helen said, white, "That's quite enough."

"I think so too," said Carol, "so, if you're ready —" she smiled a little, because now she was so sure, now all the pieces of the pattern fell into place and made sense — "shall we join the gentlemen?" she asked.

152

They went into the living room in silence. But Carol's heart beat quickly and her cheeks were red and her stormy eyes were clear. Because she had looked at Miles before he had known she was there, and she had seen only embarrassment. She had seen, the moment he knew of her presence, and Adam's, relief. He may not have known it but he had been glad that they had come.

Helen looked from her husband to Miles. She said, with a pretty humility:

"I'm so sorry — to make such an idiot of myself at my age!"

"It's the right age for it," said Adam and she would have been happy to walk to the chair for his murder at that moment. He touched her shoulder. He said, "Let's go downstairs and get a drink. It's a nice little bar and a compromise between going home or to some gay spot, which would bore us all."

"Swell," said Miles heartily and Helen, who had opened her mouth, shut it again, into a firm line. She had rouged it, with less than her usual care. Anyone who wished could see that, its natural lines followed, it was a rather thin little mouth, though shapely enough.

So they went out and downstairs and into the bar, done lavishly in hunting scenes.

There was piped-in music, not many people, good liquor, if not too plentiful these days, and a pleasant, relaxing atmosphere.

Helen said, "I'll have some brandy — I think I need it."

"When my wife drinks," said Adam to Miles, "it's for medicinal and not social purposes."

He ordered highballs and the brandy. They sat and drank and talked of Miles' orders. And Helen said, brightly, "I've a wonderful idea. We'll open the cottage, right away, and then when Miles has weekends, he can use it. Take people down," she said vaguely, "and perhaps we can be there, too."

"Splendid," said Adam, cordially.

Carol spoke. She had her glass in her hand and now she turned it, listening to the cool little tune of the ice.

"I'm going to ask my boss for a vacation," she said. "I rate one, later, but I'd like to take it now. June's lovely at the cottage and it would be pleasant to be away from the office until the gossip dies down."

Helen's face altered but Miles and Adam looked at Carol with interest.

"What gossip, or mustn't we ask?" said her father.

She said, evenly, "You may. You'll know

soon enough, if you read the papers. Providing you can read. I am breaking my engagement," she said, and smiled at them brilliantly. "Isn't that absurd? At least, Mother thinks it is."

"It's wonderful," said Adam happily. "Congratulations, dear."

Miles' eyebrows were startled. He asked, "Are you kidding?"

"No," said Carol.

"Well, poor guy," Miles commented.

Carol laughed. "Thanks," she said, "that's one of the nicest things you've ever said to me."

Helen said, "This is hardly the time or place but . . ." The brandy was warm in her veins, both stimulating and relaxing. She drank so rarely that a little sufficed.

"But what?" asked Adam.

"But I believe Carol is making a grave mistake."

Adam said, "If she is, it's her own."

Miles said, comfortably, "Hey, maybe I ought to excuse myself and get on upstairs."

"Not at all," said Adam, "as Carol remarked recently, you're practically one of the family. And it's no secret that I've never been besotted over my exfuture son-in-law. I suppose it's partly vanity. You see," he added thoughtfully, "aside from the fact that

155

I don't like him personally, nor many of the things which he represents, I asked a favor of him last winter and he refused it."

Carol's eyes were enormous.

"A favor!" she said incredulously.

"He didn't tell you? I didn't think he would. He's a secretive egg," said Adam. "Sure, he was around a lot, I saw the way love's wind was blowing and I thought he'd incline an ear. I asked him to send me overseas as one of his war correspondents. He has half a dozen on the payroll, one more wouldn't matter. Besides, I thought I had an angle on the thing. I had approached a couple of newspapers and no dice. But *Foresight* has a large staff and a hell of a lot of money. So I thought, Dear Dudley will see that I go forth and report this war in my own way — no brass hats," he added, to his wife, "no celebrities and high commands. Just the little guy, with sore feet and a yen to come home. Mud and stuff. I thought, That's my ticket and I'll die for my country with malaria or ulcers or someone will shoot me in the pants. But little Dudley said, No. He was interested in my offer but he feared it couldn't be. He said I was too old."

"Well, damn him," said Carol sincerely, "if that's what you wanted to do."

"That's what I wanted," said Adam, "and it's still what I want. But there seem to be no other avenues. Practically every editor has his own bright busybody reporting the war in his own bright way. And most of them," he said, "are a damned sight better than I'd ever be. A lot of them have died, being better. I know that. I know my place, and it's at home," he said, "writing about young love."

Miles said, liking him better than ever before, if against his judgment, "I'm sorry, sir."

"There you go again!" said Adam, with resignation.

Helen said, her beautiful voice rough at the edges, "I think we'd better get on home, Adam."

Adam beckoned a waiter but Miles forestalled him neatly when the man came. He said, smiling, "My house, so your money's no good." He signed the check, put a tip on the plate, and rose. "I'm sorry," he said, "that you have to go, it's not late yet."

Carol said, "I'm staying."

Helen looked at her daughter. "I think you'd better come with us," she suggested.

Carol shook her dark head. She said, "No. Miles will walk me home. Meantime if he's feeling so hospitable, he can buy me another drink."

Adam took Helen by the arm. He said, "Come along, my dear and leave the young folks to their own devices." His voice was cream-smooth and she jerked her arm away. It was a harsh, impatient gesture. As a rule all her gestures flowed without hurry, they were easy and graceful.

Chapter Twelve

When they had gone, Miles and Carol sat down at the little table. He asked, mechanically, "What will it be?" and she said, "The same, only I expect I sha'n't drink it." He ordered, and when the waiter had gone asked her, surprised to discover that he was really curious, "Why did you want to stay?"

She chuckled astonishingly, "If I go home, I'll lie awake rehearsing speeches and I don't want to do that," she explained.

"Speeches? Oh, I see, Lennox. Look here," he said, "it's none of my business, but have you thought it over?"

"Certainly not," said Carol indignantly, "did you think things over out there in the Pacific when you were a fighter pilot on his job? I mean, didn't you just go — *wham!*"

"Well, something like that," he admitted, "but knocking off Japs, to say nothing of saving your own neck, is hardly comparable to breaking an engagement."

She said, "But it's likewise a momentous decision. I suppose you should come to it by prayer and fasting. I didn't. I asked myself,

159

for quite a while, 'Let me see, do I want to be engaged?' Finally, I replied, firmly, 'I do,' and then out of a practically clear sky, I said, 'No, I don't.' "

"Maybe Lennox is lucky after all. You are apparently a gal who doesn't know her own mind," said Miles thoughtfully.

She looked at him, a long, direct regard. She said, "I know my own mind now."

Miles said, "I don't know Lennox very well. But he doesn't strike me as the sort of guy who'd take this lying down."

"He won't," said Carol, without expression. "And he'll have a second in his corner."

"Who?"

"My mother."

Miles flushed, a little. He had, for a few moments, forgotten Helen. He said, uneasily, "So I gathered from something she said to me when I —" He stopped, but it was too late. Carol put her elbows on the table, and laughed. She said, "Don't tell me you actually took an interest? What did she say about us — Dudley and me?"

He said, "Oh, nothing much. Just something to the effect that I didn't think you were suited."

"Smart boy. Why?"

"Oh hell," said Miles, "I dunno. He's a lot older and he seems sort of, well, smooth and quick and — I suppose the word is experienced."

Carol asked, with delight, "And I'm a rough-hewn, deficient thyroid, and completely naïve?"

Miles scowled at her. Then he laughed. He said, "No. At first I thought you were, well, pretty poised and cool, and not-give-a-damnish — but I've changed my mind."

"I see," said Carol.

After a minute he said, "I don't believe that about your mother. I mean, if you aren't happy in this engagement she'd be the last person to urge you to stick to it. She —" he hesitated. He concluded finally, "I expect she knows a good deal about people."

Which wasn't what he had in mind. Carol knew that and could have ended the sentence for him neatly, could have said, "I expect she knows a good deal about unhappiness."

She said, "Well, forget me. Tomorrow's M day or whatever you call it. Tell me about your orders and everything. Then, finish your drink and take me home."

She wondered as they walked home and Miles talked about himself, what Adam and Helen had had to say to one another. She thought, her hand on Miles' arm, He's never talked this way before. Of course it's because he wants to talk about anything except what

161

we saw when we walked into the apartment. But still, it's a break for me. . . .

Helen and Adam had not spoken going home, except once. Then she said shortly, "I dare say you misunderstood what you saw," and he answered pleasantly, "My dear girl, considering the circumstances, I am sure there was only one interpretation," and let it go at that.

At the Hillary house Miles waited until the door was open, then he said, "Goodnight — I'll be seein' you. I understand we get into town now and then. I'll 'phone — I promised Helen —" he added quickly, "I hope you weren't upset by — by tonight."

She said, "No, of course not. I understand perfectly."

The door closed and Miles went off down the street. He wasn't sure that he liked Carol's reply, now that he thought it over. It could mean anything. It could mean just that or something else again. It could put him properly in his place, in a very unattractive situation, a man consoling a weeping woman. What was unattractive about that? Nothing except that as an audience the woman's daughter and husband left a good deal to be desired.

Adam didn't matter, especially. He was a general hell-raiser and he and Helen hadn't lived together for years by her own admission. She had guts and she had sensibility, sticking it out with him because of Carol. Yet Miles had an uneasy feeling that Carol, if consulted, might not have seen it that way. He had changed his opinion of her. She was human, and she was fun. She had her little weaknesses — the night they'd danced and she felt ill, she'd been as cross and impatient as a child. And, too, on the next night she'd been incalculable and gay and made a very direct play for him just out of high-heartedness. Maybe, he thought, because she'd made up her mind to give Lennox the air and was feeling emotionally frisky. She was a cute kid, he decided, for the first time looking upon her as younger than himself, and very good looking. Also she had what it takes. He'd experienced that at first hand, to his own surprise. Someone should warn her that she carried quite a bomb load on her own account and was a little careless about her target.

He went back to his rooms in the hotel and looked around for a moment. It had been strange to come into them, to know that he could sleep in that bed, as late as he pleased, pick up a telephone and give an order. He was used to it by now, you quickly grew accustomed.

And it would be strange to leave again and go back to the BQ life — the life of men and planes and talk and work. He wondered how long they'd keep him doing a special sort of duty on the Island, how soon before they'd ship him out to instruct further, how long before he'd be overseas again?

In a way he was glad he was going, taking at least the first step toward that distant airfield wherever it might be. He might easily have made a fool of himself. Perhaps he had. He ran a finger between his shirt collar and throat and found he was sweating. But Helen Hillary was pretty damned remarkable. She had been the first woman he had seen in a long time who made you aware of her, in that urgent way. Also she was a woman with understanding, and with actual knowledge of what this war was all about. Quite a combination. Why this sudden intimacy tonight should have thrown him off he didn't know. But it had. Perhaps if Carol and Adam hadn't barged in? Good God, he'd been hoping for days that something would happen to bring Helen close to him, emotionally, and physically. Then it had and he'd been as awkward as a kid, as embarrassed — like the nightmare that you're walking down Main Street, naked as a jay bird, from which you wake to find, by golly, that you are!

It made him sore. Possibly because he recognized suddenly, bleakly, his basic youth; because the dream is always better than the realization and because he had seen Carol standing there, very still, very white, only her eyes blazing with an expression he could not read.

He stood by his bed and absently picked up a wisp of white linen crumpled into a soft little ball. He smoothed it out and looked at it. Helen's, he supposed. But it wasn't Helen's. Across one corner the word *Carol* was embroidered in facsimile handwriting. Her handwriting, not Helen's. He had seen Helen's. This was a square blunt writing, half printing, stubborn and individual.

Automatically he raised it to his face and smelled a faint sweet fragrance, like flowers after rain.

He wondered what she thought of him. He wondered what Lennox would think when the news was broken to him, tomorrow night.

Carol wondered too. She had arranged things carefully. She had invaded Agatha's room before dinner and told her. "I'm breaking my engagement," she said.

Agatha took that calmly. She said, "Better now than when it's too late. But, as a matter

165

of curiosity, why did you rush into it?"

"I didn't think I was rushing," Carol explained. "You see, it took me six months to decide that I would marry him —"

"And how long to decide that you wouldn't?"

"Six seconds."

Agatha said, "I thought something was wrong — your father thought so too. But neither of us is the type to interfere. Personally I think Dudley is a clever young man, and quite attractive. But I have never been sure that he was right for you. However," she smiled at her great-niece, "it's a pity," she said practically, "that you bothered to announce it. All those things to send back!"

"Not as many as if I had broken it at the altar," said Carol, smiling. "Be a good egg and see me through dinner. It will be baked meat before the funeral. Father's gone off somewhere — Club, I think. Mother has announced she's dining in her room and going over her radio script with one of the girls. Don't you run out on me."

"Why should I?" said Agatha. "I never have."

Dudley arrived at the correct time and Ole had the cocktails ready. Agatha was already in the living room, alone, so he hadn't a moment with Carol before dinner. She came in, apologized, gave him her hand and withdrew it. He asked, "What, no warmer welcome for the wayfarer?"

"Plenty," she said cheerfully, "and all in the shaker — Manhattans, just as you like them."

Dinner was good. Dudley was hungry. He was also feeling rather pleased with himself, as he had run into a stroke of luck in Washington. He was amusing about the people he had seen and an important dinner he had attended. If he noticed anything unusual in Carol's manner he did not comment. As a matter of fact, Agatha thought, she is carrying it off very well.

After dinner, they went to the drawing room for coffee and Agatha lingered an appreciable time. She could not linger all evening nor would Carol expect that. Anyway, the child would want to get it over with, she thought, and so thinking, excused herself and left the room, very tall in her black frock, carrying herself like a banner.

"Well," said Dudley, "at last." He looked at Carol, sitting in a deep chair near the opened windows. "I believe the expression reads, 'alone at last.' Come here, darling."

She rose and moved toward him. And he asked quietly, "Why aren't you wearing your ring?"

He made no move to touch her. Carol sat down by the empty fireplace. She opened her little handbag and the diamond shone in her palm. She said, "Dudley, I'm sorry — but I'm not going to wear it, ever again."

He said nothing for a moment. Then he said, "You're breaking our engagement?"

"Yes."

"Why?"

She said, "I wish I had a lot of reasons. But I have only one, the most important. I find that, after all, I don't love you, Dudley."

He agreed, "No other reason counts. But isn't this rather — precipitous?" he asked.

"I suppose so." She looked at him gravely. "I wasn't sure," she said, "for a long time that I did, you know."

"I know," he said. He shrugged faintly. "That's that, isn't it?"

"I'm afraid so."

She laid the ring on a little table between them. It was very beautiful. No girl could surrender such a jewel without a pang.

He asked, "There's nothing I can say nor do?"

"Nothing. And I'm so sorry," she told him, "sorry that it had to happen, sorry that it must be this way — and sorry too that we announced it — if I'd only waited . . ."

He said with a touch of impatience, "The

minor details don't interest me, Carol, what matters is that I love you and you're lost to me. Will you tell me one thing honestly?"

She said, "Of course," hoping that she need not.

"Is there anyone else?"

She was compelled to answer, and truly. She said, "Yes."

"Will you tell me — who?"

She shook her head. She said, and tried to smile, "I'd rather not. You see, we're on the same side of the fence, you and I. Because I'm not in love with you any more, and he never has been, with me."

"I see." He was silent. Then he asked, "Have you told your family?"

"Yes."

"And?"

She said, "Mother's angry with me, she's always liked you. Father and Aunt Agatha — well, whatever I decide, it's all right with them."

He rose and picked up the ring and put it in his pocket, carelessly. It was a lot of stone to carry that way. He moved quickly, and lifted her from her chair and kissed her hard, with a calculated anger and a calculated harshness, and with passion which was not calculated at all. When he released her she stood back, white, and very quiet. And he said, presently:

"You understand, I accept only the outward form of this. I release you of course, although," he added, "you haven't asked me to, it seems. You're a trifle highhanded. I like it. I like spirit in a woman. There have been times when I've thought you lacked it. So I'm warning you, I don't accept this gracefully, I don't bow to the inevitable and I certainly don't want to be your elder brother nor your trusted friend. I want to be your lover and your husband and I intend to be, if I have to wait a long time. I don't know who this other man is, I cannot," he added, quite untruthfully, "imagine, and I don't particularly care. For, whoever he is, you'll get over him, and you'll come back to me, Carol — you'll come back!"

Chapter Thirteen

The Hillary cottage on Long Island was not in a fashionable or publicized section. Helen had bought the place some years ago and Adam, much against his will, liked it very much. It was typical of Helen to avoid the dowager, diamond and dunes atmosphere of Southampton, or the gayer aura of Easthampton, and find herself a charming if almost isolated hideout.

The village was reached by side roads from the excellent highway or by a slow, crawling, local train. It was really a village, it had a general store which also accommodated the U.S. mails, a gas station, a drugstore and a few weather-beaten frame residences. Side roads wandered off into the country and ran whimsically past truck farms, and to the bright blue water, between acres of scrub pine and oak.

The property had once been a real estate development, in the days of the First World War. It had been surveyed and advertised and financed on a shoestring. Only a few people had bought lots of varying acreage and built homes. These had passed through various hands, including those of the banks, and when Helen chanced upon the locality, all but three or four of the houses were for sale.

She bought, at bargain rates, the best property in the development, with considerable acreage running out on a point above the curving bay. The house was good, simple, the Adirondack lodge type. Later, she bought the adjoining land to protect herself and now owned about twenty-five acres, mostly in woods, underbrush and sand. She had made no attempt to glorify the place to the stature of an estate. There was no garden, no swimming pool, no stables and no staff. The other houses, none nearby, had been closed for the duration and a caretaker, Mr. Griffin, whose salary was underwritten by all the owners, looked after things, and rattled out every so often from the village in his ancient Ford. When the Hillarys wished to come down for a week or a week-end, they telephoned him and he saw that the house was opened and aired, and comfortable.

Helen, together with her neighbors, kept up the private road leading from the country road, to some extent. It wasn't much of a road, but it was passable. Its condition discouraged droppers-in, she said, at all times, and especially during the war, that is, if they had any respect for their tires. Supplies came from the general store, and you walked to the village for your mail if you were sparing of gas.

She had seen to it that the place was comfortable, if without luxury, and that the necessities were there. An artesian well supplied plentiful, wonderful water, and electricity had been brought in by the original real estate company. There was, however, no telephone. She could have had one at any time before the war but preferred not to — it was the one place in the world, she explained, where she could not be reached except in an emergency. If such arose, her secretaries and family knew that they could call Mr. Griffin at the general store and he would send word in to her.

A succession of pleasant local girls or women were, or had been, available for daily work, cleaning and cooking. Mr. Griffin arranged that too. And there was a heating plant which assured warmth during the cool springs and on autumn weekends.

It was a lovely, quiet place, so undisturbed most of the time that the little woods were bright and vocal with birds, squirrels and chipmunks who chattered about their business near the house and all the busy, secret life of the trees and undergrowth went on uninterrupted.

Carol came to the cottage on a bright June morning. She had asked for her vacation and it had been given to her without question. The meager announcement of the abrogation of her engagement had appeared in the press and there had been some bee-buzzing columnist speculation, but not much. Most of the reportorial questioning came to Helen, who neatly evaded it. She had nothing to say except that her daughter and Mr. Lennox had reached an agreement.

Miles was at Mitchel Field, and Helen, having worked furiously with her secretaries for several days, had turned the slim manuscript over to Frank Whitney and gone off on a lecture tour. She had heard from Miles, she said vaguely, the day before she left. But Carol heard from him too. He telephoned her one evening from the Field. He was, he said, busy, and restless. He might come to town soon. How about a date?

She answered, as calmly as possible under the circumstances that she was going to the Island.

He might, he told her, borrow a car and get a day off and come see her. Where was the place, how did one reach it?

She told him that too, her heart hammering, and the conversation was concluded.

The night before she left for the Island, Frank Whitney dropped by for a drink with Adam. He liked Adam very much, now that the old feeling of guilt had worn down, eroded by the years, and was no longer a notable bump in the territory of his conscience. Carol came in while they were sitting over their highballs and Whitney looked at her and grinned. He said, "You do things in a hurry."

She admitted it, smiling a little, and Whitney shook his head. He said, "Your mother's very unhappy about it, Carol."

"That can't be helped," said Carol cheerfully, and accepted a small drink from the hands of her father.

Whitney said thoughtfully, "I'm worried about Helen."

Adam glanced up. "Why?" he inquired.

"The Duncan yarn," said Whitney, "it isn't much good. That is, it's an excellent straightforward, workmanlike story and it will sell, because all such stories sell. But it lacks — something. Helen can take a simple adventure, even an ordinary experience and lift it into excitement. Not that she's ever been a novelist. But she has the novelist's slang and everything she's ever done shows

175

it. Except this. Any bright young woman, any good reporter, any sympathetic person with a gift for words could have written this book. I dare say Duncan himself could have done it — and better. Which worries me because I am wondering how good her own book will be —"

Helen was writing the story of her last trip to China and beyond. She was writing it in trains and hotel rooms, she was writing it on planes, if she had a plane priority, and in the dreary places where priority ended and she was put off to wait for a train. She had had her notes all assembled upon her return, but Miles' story had been more immediate so she had set aside her own story until she had finished with that. Now, she was at it again. It was promised within a few weeks and would be rushed through as fast as possible under present conditions. It would reach book publication before Miles' story, for she had refused to sell the magazine rights, and Miles had sold his.

"It is possible," said Adam carelessly, "that she lost her first fine fervor of enthusiasm for her subject." He grinned. He thought he knew the answer. There was too much Fighter Pilot, it was all Miles and would have nothing of Helen Hillary in it.

Carol said, "Perhaps you've lost your enthusiasm, Frank. There are so many war books."

He looked into his empty glass, and said merely, "There's something odd about it . . ." He glanced at Adam. "How's your yarn going?" he asked. "Not that I give a damn, I sit and gnash what's left of my teeth in envy — but just to show I appreciate hospitality."

"Badly," said Adam glumly, "if it's any consolation to you. I have half a mind to scrap the whole thing and take a defense plant job. I'd be a lot more contented, I believe, and at any rate, more useful."

Carol excused herself. She had to pack, she said. And when Frank asked, "Why?" she answered that she was going down to the cottage for a couple of weeks. "Maybe I'll write a book too," she told him. "*Essays in Idleness*, by Mlle. Thoreau."

The trip down was slow and dusty and the train stopped at practically every tree. The seats were faded red plush and very hot, and cinders rattled against windows streaked by recent rain. Carol loved every minute of it. Summer was fresh and green on the Island and now and then there were glimpses of far water and occasionally the curving bays crept close and there were little bridges and boys fishing from them. The fruit trees had shed their blossom-snow and their new small leaves were bright. At one stop she looked out to a yard crowded with white ducks squawking busily in the sunlight.

When she reached the station she stopped to talk to the station master, who was an old friend. His daughter, Jesse, had gone to the cottage a few days before and turned it out, and everything was in readiness. They talked about Jessie's sister, now in training in the Southampton hospital, and about the girls' mother, for many years an invalid, and then because there'd be no train coming through for quite a spell, he carried her suitcase across the street to Mr. Griffin's store.

It was a charming place. You could furnish almost anything with its contents, a modest house, a cabin cruiser, or your heart. It smelled of rope, salt, cheese, pickles, cinnamon drops, kerosene, peppermints. Mr. Griffin outfitted boats, supplied summer visitors and had an all-year-round trade as well. He sold piece and canned goods, soft, bottled drinks, candy, fishing tackle, stove oil, dishes, glasses, hair nets, fresh fish and a little meat. He sold bread and cheese, and gave good advice, gratis. He had once sold tires and stoves as well.

He had Carol's supplies ready in cartons. The old Ford was practically hitched to a post and rarin' to go. Griffin shook Carol's hand and allowed as how she looked a little peaked. What was she doing down alone, where were Helen and Agatha and Adam?

Carol reported, Helen was lecturing, Agatha busy with Red Cross and Adam couldn't come. So she came alone.

Griffin shook his gray head. He was small, very brown, very lined, very wiry. He said, he didn't like it. Away off alone like that and not a near neighbor — nobody had opened a danged house on the Point this summer and weren't likely to — and no 'phone. Suppose something went wrong, suppose she was taken sick?

She said, she wouldn't be.

"Jessie would come to stay with you," he suggested.

But she didn't want Jessie nor anyone else. She compromised finally. If she got tired of being alone and cooking her own meals, she'd walk in and let him know. It wasn't much of a walk, just three miles, she reminded him.

He said, "How are you off for points? I saved some ham for you and Minnie cooked it. You can have it cold or fry it. Got a little steak too — and some beans, and soup and the rest of the stuff you ordered. I don't have much gas," he said, shaking his head, "but I could manage to come out every two, three days and bring supplies. Got lots of milk for you, to start with, anyway.

He loaded up the Ford and presently they set off. They followed the country road for a little way, then turned off and lurched along the private road to the cottage. "It don't get much better," said Mr. Griffin critically.

Pines and oaks, the smell of fallen needles and dark soil, the smell of salt wind and of small, unseen flowers. Carol took off her hat and smiled. There was an other-worldly look to the arching sky and as the road curved you could see the water. A jay, azure, mauve and white flew, screaming, across the rutted dirt road. A robin spoke warningly, a blue-bird looked down from a branch, his breast a clear, soft rose. Somewhere a thrush sang and the sparrows scolded. It was knee-deep in peace here and the air was crystal clear and wonderful.

She thought, If Miles were only here.

She said, suddenly, "Look, Mr. Griffin, if an army officer stops at the store and asks directions to the cottage —"

"I won't give 'em?" he inquired.

Her color rose, bright. She said, "On the

contrary, give him the very best directions you have in stock."

He asked, "Army officer, eh? What branch?"

"Air Force. Fighter pilot," she said, "back from the Pacific."

He said, "We ain't heard from Rob in some time. You know he's on a submarine."

Rob was Griffin's grandson. Carol nodded. She said, "You'll hear soon."

"Yep, that's what I tell Minnie." He was silent a moment. He said presently, "I thought you were getting married."

She said, "I was. To Dudley Lennox. It's all off, now."

"I read about the engagement," he said, "in the paper. I meant to write, but I ain't much of a hand at it. Glad I didn't. It would have been a waste of paper and ink. This aviator, now — where does he fit in?"

"Major," she said, "Major Miles Duncan. He's a friend. Mother came back with him on the clipper. They met during her last trip. She's been helping him with a book about his experiences. He's stationed on the Island now, and I told him, if he could get here, how to reach me. Through you, that is."

"I'll keep my eyes peeled," said Mr. Griffin as the Ford bounced over the last curve and stopped in a clearing which was all there was of a yard.

The house was long and low, built of logs with the bark on. Helen had added to it, but the effect was not one of addition, merely of a house which had grown naturally.

The woods marched close. Carol and Mr. Griffin went in the back door, he had the keys which Jessie had returned to him. He put the things down on the kitchen table and started to unpack them. The kitchen was bright with yellow walls, checkered blue curtains. It was compact. It utilized the electricity — in range, ice box, small dishwasher. The sink was polished metal. The windows shone. Jessie had done a good job.

While Mr. Griffin unpacked and put things away, Carol walked through the house. She loved it. She and Adam had used it far more than Helen. Helen was fond of it, as she had created it, but she never seemed to find much time for it. She referred to it as her sanctuary and added that it would be a good place to go when she was old and had nothing else to do.

The living room was very large, and an open porch ran the length of the house beyond it. The room itself was simply done, with sturdy, utilitarian furniture and chintz which had faded beautifully. It was really part of the porch. And because the house was set on a little rise of land, the porch looked down to the Point and across the bay. The land dropped off beyond it, and the pines had been cut so that you had a straight clear view to the steep overgrown bank, with the stunted trees leaning against the prevailing wind to the curving white and gold beach and the water. The water was bright emerald and pale jade green in the shallows and a deep, wonderful blue beyond. The little pines had a precarious foothold on the bank and there were straggling vines of purple beach peas, and waving grasses.

There was no dining room, but a gate-legged table near the kitchen end served, together with a comfortable, old fashioned tea-wagon.

There were four bedrooms, two with a bath between, off the living room, and two more, with another bath for guests in the little wing Helen had added. It was adequate. She, Adam and Carol were rarely there together. None of these rooms was large and each contained a comfortable bed, a dresser and two chairs. The wind came through the opened windows and the pine branches stirred nearby.

Helen had made one concession to vanity in her bathroom, which had a built-in dressing table and good mirrors.

Mr. Griffin called. He asked, "Want I should bring in your suitcase?"

Carol, standing at the windows of what was tacitly Helen's bedroom, said, "Yes, in here, please." The room was the largest and pleasantest and a French window opened to the porch from it. You undressed here for your swim and went out to the porch, down the steps and along the steep, winding path to the water. She thought, I'll put on a bathing suit and spend all day there tomorrow — right after breakfast. I'll pack a lunch and take some books and find a sheltered place and read and sleep, and maybe go for a swim.

And perhaps, try to think.

Mr. Griffin lingered, reluctant to depart. She made him and herself a cup of tea and they drank it sociably in the kitchen and ate some of the ginger cookies that his wife, the Postmistress, had sent. When he left it was with a warning that he didn't like it at all and that if she was scared in the night she must walk out first thing in the morning and he'd see to it that Jessie would return with her.

It was darkening when he left. Carol unpacked her suitcase — she had brought only slacks, sweaters, the necessary things — and went out on the porch. The afterglow stained the water and gulls were screaming from the beach. She thought, If Miles were here . . .

But he wasn't and she dared not hope that he would be.

She scrambled eggs for supper, made coffee, fried potatoes, ate some of Mrs. Griffin's ineffable angel food cake and sat a long time over her cigarette. Tomorrow, she thought, she would fix breakfast on a tray and carry it out on the porch. Lunch on the beach, and early supper, while it was still light, also on the porch. And early to bed.

She had not known how tired she was, how much tension possessed her nerves and slender body, until she reached the cottage, felt the wind and sun on her face and listened to the pines talking. She thought, I can get myself together here, I can relax . . .

She washed up, turned out the lights in the kitchen and living room and went to bed. Agatha had supplied her with some mystery novels. "Good and gory," said Agatha, "if you're like me you don't scare easily, they'll just put you to sleep."

But she couldn't read much after the first few chapters, her eyes grew heavy and she turned out her light and slept. She woke in the night, a drowsy bird spoke close by, and she heard the little steps of an animal — a woodchuck, a skunk? Yes, definitely a skunk, she thought, smiling, and went back to sleep again.

The next day dawned blue and gold. Carol woke early and lay listening to the awakening life of the woods and beach. She thought, I should go for a swim, and shivered thinking about it. After a while she rose with reluctance and presently, in brief bathing shorts, a halter and play shoes, she slung a towel around her shoulders and went out on the porch and down the bank.

The beach was marked with the imprints of delicate bird feet, where the tide had receded and left the brown wet sand. A twisted beach palm grew quite near. There were yellow shells, fragile as fingernails. There were little pebbles and a ruffle of foam and everywhere you looked there was only sky and brilliant water and sunlight, only trees and birds flying, except, across the bay, a solitary fisherman, motionless in an anchored boat.

The water was cold as calamity on her feet and she drew back and stood there, hesitating. But the sun rose steadily and it was warm and the little wind sighed and dropped. She drew a deep breath, waded out and ducked, like a child. The clear coolness bracing with salt flowed over her from head to feet. She had forgotten to bring a cap and you couldn't buy one anywhere for love or money. She gasped and rose to the surface and swam out with strong, steady strokes.

She came in after a time and sat in the sun to dry her hair and then ran back to the house. She stood on the porch and dropped her halter and shorts. No one was there to see. If the weather grew warmer she would swim naked, she thought, at night under the stars and in the early morning.

She wrapped a quilted robe about her, an old one which hung with sweaters and fishing gear and hip boots and heaven knew what else in a closet, and went to the kitchen to start the coffee. Then she rinsed the salt from her hair and sat out on the porch, drying it, until the coffee was ready. And then, still in the thick robe, she carried her crazy, satis-factory breakfast to the rustic table on the porch and ate it looking out over the water — coffee, a glass of milk, ginger cookies and an apple.

It was a good day, mint new, and she loved it. She spent it in utter laziness and dream-ing, under the pines, on the beach with sand-wiches, fruit and a thermos nearby. She spent it reading and sleeping and going in for a swim when the sun was at its height. She spent it looking over fishing tackle and planning to have Mr. Griffin bring the boat down out of the shed the next time he came. She might paint it, she thought; it probably leaked.

Also she spent it thinking of Miles. And all the clamor and excitement and uncertainty was washed from her by the sun and wind and water. Things became clear and direct and simple. She was in love with him. If this were "just" physical attraction, it sufficed. She wanted to be with him, she wanted to sleep and wake with him, she wanted to wait for him wherever he might go, afraid, because she loved him, yet because she loved him, unafraid.

Loving him, if she could open his eyes to that loving, if by some miracle she could make him love her in return, she would do so. There was no shame in this, no immodesty of the mind. It was very simple. It was not unusual, she told herself, as it had been going on since first man and first woman. It would continue.

If Miles came to her, this minute, across the white and gold and faintly rosy sand and sat down beside her and said, "You know, Carol, I thought I was in love with your mother," she would put her sun-warm hand on his and say, "Of course you were, dear . . ." Because he wasn't really, he hadn't been, he couldn't be. It wasn't a question of Helen's seniority, it was a question of Helen herself. You could fall in love with her but you didn't love her. She was a light which dazzled the eyes and passed.

The day passed too and Carol went back to the house, put on slacks and a sweater and looked over her larder. Mr. Griffin had saved her a very fine steak indeed. There was no use keeping it and she was hungry. It was well worth the points it had cost, a beautiful steak, the fat and the lean companionable.

Coffee, and the rest of the potatoes she had boiled for frying last night, creamed. Bread and butter, jam and a green salad. She was grateful to Aunt Agatha who had taught her to cook. Aunt Agatha had said, "A woman who can't do everything that her hired help does is an utterly useless and futile person — and open to blackmail. I taught your mother and I'm going to teach you."

It was still light, the long, lingering light of early summer. She would be able to take her supper out on the porch. She was looking at the steak sizzling in the broiler when she heard the car. She thought, Mr. Griffin — and was half annoyed, half amused. Old fuss-

189

budget! If he had brought Jessie, she would kill him.

The car stopped. And a voice called, "Hi, anyone home?"

It was Miles . . .

She shut the door of the range carefully, thinking for a moment that she had gone crazy, that only a longing for that particular voice had produced it in her wayward ears. But Miles called again. He asked, "Carol, where are you?" and then he was at the back door.

She opened it and stood looking at him and he grinned at her and asked, "Am I in time for supper?"

"Of course." She was sedate and quiet suddenly. This was magic, as a fairy story is magic and you must react as if such visitations were of everyday, and not sheer enchantment. She said, "The steak's almost ready."

He came in and dropped the small bag he was carrying. He said, "It smells good, and I'm starved. I got away late, and I got lost." He put his arm around her shoulder. He added, "I've missed you."

"That's good," she said.

"You aren't surprised to see me? What a girl. I tried to 'phone you before I left. No dice, because no 'phone. I called New York

190

— and Ole said, nobody home. I couldn't remember the name of the man who ran the general store — but knew if I found it there'd be only one. Find it I did, after various adventures, involving rustic maidens, chipmunks and, of all things, a flat tire. Anyway I discovered the store and your Mr. Griffin. He wasn't too cordial. He said you were alone. However, he directed me, and kept me waiting while he wrote you a note. Here it is, the seal unbroken. He didn't trust me," said Miles.

She said, "Wait till I set the table — we'll sit out on the porch."

She put the envelope in her pocket and turned her back on Miles. Her cheeks were too bright and her eyes, and her heart beat too quickly. She removed her steak, slid a platter under it, and directed her guest. Cups, saucers, plates, glasses, silverware. She loaded a tray and ordered, "Go straight through the living room."

When the table was set, she looked at him. She said, "Run, find yourself a bathroom, and wash — and hurry."

She sat waiting, and while she waited she read Mr. Griffin's letter. Mr. Griffin said plump and plain that he had tried to get hold of Jessie when the young man turned up. But Jessie had gone away for the day and evening. When the Major left, if Carol had any directions for him, Mr. Griffin, the Major was to stop by the house.

She smiled and put the note back in her pocket.

Miles came out. He said, "This is a wonderful house, the kind you dream about. I have dreamed about it, as a matter of fact. Helen told me about it, a world away. It didn't seem possible then that a place like this still existed. She told me how she had stumbled across it and what she had done to it."

A little chill crept across the warmth of Carol's spirit. She said, "Eat your steak and potatoes, Miles, before they are cold."

He ate, smiling at her. He said, "I could stay here for weeks. I have, by the way, a couple of days. It was one of those breaks which don't often happen . . ." He looked at her a moment and raised an eyebrow. He added, "I didn't see a hotel."

"There isn't one," said Carol, "and you know it."

He said, mildly — and somehow reminded her of her father:

"I gathered that both from personal observation and Mr. Griffin. He told me, by the way, that he'd be glad to put me up."

Carol said evenly, "It isn't necessary,

192

Miles. There's plenty of room here. If you can stand my cooking I'll be glad to have you stay."

He said, "I hoped you'd say that. But I wasn't sure. As a matter of fact I thought maybe Miss Stuart was down here with you until I saw Griffin."

"Aunt Agatha hates the place," said Carol. "She's a born Cockney. The country scares the daylights out of her, it's too noisy."

He said, after a moment, "Look — if you have the least hesitation about this —?"

"Should I have?" she asked, smiling. "Do I look like Little Red Riding Hood?"

He said seriously, "Not very much. But your father or Miss Stuart might cry 'Wolf'!"

"Why," she asked, "do you exclude Mother?"

He looked uneasy. He said, "I didn't mean to . . ."

Carol laughed. She felt like laughing, it was true laughter, and gay. She said, "We're both grown up, I doubt if you have designs on me." She looked at him, "And if I have any on you, they don't include seduction," she concluded.

"Carol!"

"Or do they?" she asked, very much entertained by his expression of shock. "At any rate, we won't stop to argue that now." She rose. "Angel food," she asked, "or ginger cookies? There's fruit too and if I had known you were coming I would have made an apple pie."

"You can really cook?" he asked, incredulously.

"Did you think little green men prepared this repast?" she inquired — and departed, leaving him looking out over the water and the pines.

When she came back he asked, "Is there fishing?"

"Of course, there's always fishing. You won't get anything very startling this time of year but maybe you'll find a blackfish or two," she answered, "and they're wonderful eating. We can carry the boat down from the shed, and see how much it leaks."

"I'll sleep late," he told her, "and go for a swim . . ." He looked startled. "Only I haven't any trunks . . ."

She said, "You won't need 'em. I promise to stay off the beach and when later in the day you decide you'd like company, I'll find a pair of Father's for you. They'll be much too big but we'll anchor them with a safety pin."

He said, reverently, "You think of everything. By the way, what did your friend Mr. Griffin say in the letter?"

She said, "He doesn't, of course, approve. But he won't do anything about it unless I ask him to. If I ask, if, that is, I send you back to the village tonight, he'll offer you bed and even board, he'll find us a chaperone, he'll do everything. If I don't ask, he'll stay out of things. He'll be curious but he won't gossip. And he won't interfere because he respects other people's decisions and admits their right to live as they please. He doesn't have to applaud their methods but he doesn't try to reform them. Besides, I flatter myself that he knows and likes me well enough to be troubled only by the routine conventional aspect of this adventure."

Miles said, "I suppose I didn't think too much about that — you get out of the habit."

She said, rising, "And now, you'll get into the habit of dish washing. If you're staying here you have to pull your weight in the boat. No loafers allowed. Come help me clear away," she ordered, "and then I'll show you your room."

He asked, following her to the kitchen, "Do I have to go to bed now, Grandma?"

"No," she said, "unless you'd rather. We'll build a fire in the living room and sit and talk for a while. I'm sorry I haven't a drink to offer you. Adam never leaves any liquor here."

"Only a slight flaw," he murmured.

In the kitchen, he watched her as she washed their dishes. Her hair curled, riotously, without benefit of hairdresser. Her face was rosy from the sun, and unpowdered, and she wore no lipstick. He thought, suddenly, that she was as pretty a girl as he had ever seen. He said so, after a fashion. He said, "I like you scrubbed up like this."

Carol scowled, briefly. She said, "You caught me with my lipstick off. It's something I shall never forgive. It will, however, teach me not to believe myself alone in the wilderness."

She thought, watching him handle the dishes with awkward care, I have two days, and two nights.

Chapter Fourteen

After their dishes were washed they went back to the living roof. Mr. Griffin had filled the wood box and Miles built a fire. He put a match to it and a brief flame flared. "See," he said in triumph, "boy scout stuff."

Carol, in the corner of the big shabby couch, applauded dutifully, and then the flame died down. Amused, she watched him struggle with the logs and the kindling. He stabbed his finger on a sharp splinter and swore, and Carol grinned, restraining herself from rising and kicking the logs briskly into place with an experienced and competent toe. Let him struggle, she thought, and when he achieves what he's after, enjoy it.

She remembered Adam's counsel, bestowed upon her long ago when she was going through the stress of her first grown-up love affair. He'd said, "Carol, let me give you a tip. The women men like are friendly, human and warm. They have pleasant flaws and charming weaknesses. They are competent in the important things, the ordering of a household, the creating of a satisfactory meal. But when they become too competent in realms which men have long considered their bailiwicks, it's best to hide it — except in an emergency. Contrary to general opinion, men don't dislike clever women. They merely dislike women who aren't clever enough to conceal their cleverness. Nor are they, as a rule, fond of witty women — they're scared of them. They don't want their women dumb, in the accepted sense of the word, but there are times when they like 'em mute. And such women, with an instinct for selfless loving win over all competitors, hands down."

Miles got his fire going, dusted his hands absently along the seams of his slacks and grinned. He said, "There she blows."

Presently he came to sit beside Carol. He put his arm around her and commented, "You're a very comfortable person . . ."

Carol said nothing but her breath and her heartbeat seemed suspended. He kissed her lightly, experimentally, and then drew her closer. He said, in a loud and startled voice, "But damned exciting, too," and kissed her again, the reverse of lightly.

Carol put her arms around his neck. She was no niggardly lover, but generous and surrendering. When Miles released her he was conscious of chilly fingers up and down his spine, and a vast astonishment.

"For Pete's sake!" he said helplessly.

Carol laughed; the laughter was low and shaken. She said, unsteadily:

"You asked for it."

"Sure," he admitted, "but I didn't bargain for . . ." He broke off. "Woman," he asked, "did I dream that, just now? How about kissing me again to make sure?"

Carol shook her head, a gesture which cost her much in self discipline. She said, firmly, "No —"

"Why not?" he demanded.

She answered gently, and very quietly, "It wouldn't be fair."

"To whom?"

"To us both." She added, without a change of expression, "You see, I'm very much in love with you."

His reply was utterly unromantic, as automatic as the ringing of a telephone and as genuine as bread and butter.

"Are you *kidding?*" he demanded, incredulously.

"No," said Carol.

Miles hunted for a cigarette, found a battered pack and set a match to the only one it contained. He said:

"Well, if you're not, you're crazy."

"That's right," she said, "crazy enough to

break all the rules, at least."

"Rules?"

"You know. Be coy — horrible word — never pursue, be the hunted, not the hunter. Personally, I think that's stupid. Everyone knows that women do the hunting. Only men prefer to think they do." She was laughing now, with authentic amusement, at his expression. "Darling," she said, "don't look like that. You aren't committed to anything — not even a lunatic asylum."

He said, slowly, "I think I'd like to be committed. I enjoy your particular form of insanity. It's catching."

He seized her, suddenly, kissed her, hard and long — and released her. "One for the book," he murmured, "and it's still there, by golly."

"What is?"

"The — the comfortableness and the excitement. Maybe I've fallen in love with you too," he added, bewildered, "because there's something very different about this —"

"Different from what?"

"Other times," he said vaguely.

"Nonsense," Carol told him cheerfully, "in the morning you will have thought things over and you'll be headed back to the field as fast as tires and gas can take you."

There was the catch. He might. Very easily, he might. Yet she felt that, in justice, she should provide him with a blueprint for escape.

He said, "But you were in love with Lennox."

"I thought so," she admitted, "but was never quite sure.

"And you're sure now?"

She said, "It doesn't make sense but I've never been as sure of anything, from the first moment . . ."

"When was that?" he wondered.

"The night we went out and danced —"

He said, "So that was it."

"What?"

"Nothing . . . Everything." He hesitated. He said, "But you — before you met Lennox?"

"You mean was I ever in love before. Oh, now and then. It was never quite real. Even when I told Dudley I'd marry him."

He said, "You're the most honest person I've ever known. I — well, gosh, there have been girls. Not that *I* ever thought I was in love, exactly. You wouldn't know about that, or," he asked, suddenly, "would you?"

She said quietly, "If you mean have I ever had an affair, no, Miles, I wouldn't know."

He was scarlet, and it wasn't entirely the reflection of the firelight. He said:

201

"I didn't mean — well, perhaps I did. I'm sorry, Carol, I had no right . . ."

"Every right in the world. Stop chewing on that cigarette. Throw it away, it's disgusting. Here, take my case." She gave it to him, smiling. "Now that that's settled, let's talk about the Field. Tell me what you're doing, how you like it, if you've run into anyone you know and everything that's happened." And then when he still hesitated, turning the fresh cigarette between his lean fingers, she exclaimed, "Oh, for heaven's sake — at ease!"

Miles laughed. He said, "You're pretty wonderful." He put his arm around her, companionably. The astonishment had passed, and the excitement, yet they were still there, underneath, an undercurrent. He asked, "One thing first. Did you break your engagement to Lennox because of me?"

"Naturally," she responded promptly. "Don't be a dope."

He shook his head. He said, "I'll never understand you."

"That's good," said Carol, "I'd hate to be understood. Too dreary."

He said, "Lennox must hate my guts."

"Don't flatter yourself. He doesn't know. He's beating his brains out trying to find out who — because when he asked me if there was someone else I said, yes."

He said, "You're the damnedest girl. Does anyone else — ?"

"Father," she murmured, "suspects — and, possibly Mother."

She felt his arm shift, on her shoulder. He said, "They won't like it."

"Father will," she said. "He likes you. He's never cared much for Dudley. Mother —" she stopped, said a short silent prayer and then went on steadily, "Mother won't be pleased. She rather looks on you as her property."

He said uneasily, "It's a funny thing to be saying to you, Carol, but I suspect I made a damned fool of myself in that direction."

"No," she said, gravely. "She's — a pretty glamorous person. She had all the advantages, Miles."

He said, slowly, "After the places I'd been and the things I'd seen — and done, you can't imagine what it was like, meeting her —"

"I can imagine perfectly."

"Do you remember," he asked her, "the days when people talked about crushes? I had a crush on a grade school teacher once. She was awfully pretty, she liked kids and understood them. I suppose I suffered over her more than any woman I've met since.

She married some insurance guy in town and I thought hanging too good for him. Maybe it was something like that," he said, "if you get me."

"I get you," she said.

He was silent. Then he said, conversationally, "I've no business marrying you, Carol."

The room turned upside down. When the earth ceased to tremble and the house righted itself, she said, "I didn't know that you contemplated it."

"I didn't, until a few minutes ago," he told her, "and then I knew that if I could —" His arm tightened about her. He asked, "Would you? Would you take all the risks and anxiety and the lack of promises? For I couldn't promise you anything —" he paused and added, "darling." He liked it. He said it again. "Not even a future, darling," he told her.

She said, steadily, "Of course, I understand that, Miles. I'm not interested in a future. None of us can afford to be, I suppose. But we have — now."

He said, unhappily, "That's what you think. But how long is — now?"

She said, "We don't know that either. Miles, are you proposing to me, by any chance?"

"I'm afraid so," he told her.

She said, "Well, I won't have it. I'm not going to have you waking up, come tomorrow, and asking yourself, How the hell will I get out of this? Suppose we talk about something else . . . Are you satisfied with your book?"

He said, impatiently, "Oh, it's all right, I guess. I never thought I knew anything worth telling — the things I know best I couldn't tell. Carol, *why* won't you?"

She said, "If you still feel the same way when your next order comes, I'll follow you wherever you go and we'll be married and then when you go off again —" she shrugged. "I'll get a job," she said, "and wait for you."

"Is that the way you want it?"

"That's the way. I don't want it," she said, "on the strength — or weakness — of a kiss, and firelight, and being alone like this —"

He said, "Maybe you're right." He was silent a moment. Then he said, "But I don't think so. Perhaps I'm not very used to being in love yet . . ."

"That's where I have a slight advantage," she reminded him.

"I suppose you'll throw that up to me," he told her, "all the rest of our lives."

The blood sang in her ears, and the tears were hot, and immediate, back of her eyes. She closed her eyelids against them. Then she said, shakily, "No, but you will. You'll say, 'You fell in love with me first and were shameless about it. You even told me so.' And you'll tell the children, 'Your mother proposed to me . . .' which will be a base lie, because, after all, I didn't."

"Oh hush," he said, and laid his urgent mouth on hers, "you talk entirely too much —"

The firelight flickered on the walls and the fire spoke to itself in a hurried, busy little whisper. It was a very quiet night. You could hear the water and the pines, talking — you could hear the silence and the darkness . . .

After a while he said, gently, "Carol?"

She pulled herself away from him. She said, "No, darling. I'm not being — that hideous word again — coy. I'm not trying to hold you by withholding. Please believe that. And I do love you — completely. I wouldn't be sorry, I'd never be sorry. But you might be. And I'm not going to put you in a position where you'll feel obliged to go all chivalrous and conventional — tomorrow. Besides," she said very softly, "if you find — if we both find — that we want each other, not just tonight but always?"

He put his hand over her mouth. He said, a little roughly, "Okay, you win."

The tension in her nerves relaxed. She

said, "Let's go out in the kitchen and get a bottle of milk and some cookies. I think I'm hungry."

They sat for a long time in the kitchen, with the milk and the cookies on the bare table, talking. They talked about themselves. They talked about all sorts of silly, unrelated things — the big back yard in which Miles had played in Portland — the rocks and wild coastline of the summer place his people had had, the red-headed kid who had licked him in his first fight. They talked about his parents and his grandmother —" She was a little like your great-aunt," he said. 'They talked about his training, his friends, and a little about his combat experience. They talked about Carol's boarding school and his prep school and discovered that they had been not more than thirty miles apart. They talked themselves hoarse, trying to compress twenty-three, twenty-four years in an hour, two hours, three.

It was very late and the fire slept into embers, the wind spoke softly at the windows and Miles yawned, prodigiously. Carol rose, ran water in the milk bottle, washed the cookie plate and the glasses. She was so tired that she felt as if she had been beaten. She was so happy that she felt she must weep or die. She couldn't walk another step without her knees collapsing. Yet she could walk a hundred miles, now, this minute, if he were with her.

She said, "For heaven's sake, *will* you go to bed!"

She took him into the guest wing. Jessie had made up all the beds, which is, Carol thought, a break, for if I had to make one up now I'd fall screaming to the floor. And then, after she had locked up and turned out the lights, she went back to his room. She stood there in the doorway, a dark girl with tumbled hair, and shadows under her eyes and her mouth the shape of a kiss. She said, "Goodnight, darling," and put her arms around him and he bent his tall head and kissed her, gently. He said, "I don't know how it all happened or why — but it has."

She smiled, waved her hand and was gone. And a little later, fell, exhausted, into bed. She lifted her heavy lids and looked through the gray square which was the window into darkness beyond and tried to think. She must remember, every word, every gesture, every touch. She must relive it, each minute, and now. But her eyes closed and she slept, deeply, without dreams.

Chapter Fifteen

In the morning she woke, and waking, remembered. She jumped out of bed and ran to the windows and the sun was shining and it was nine o'clock. She thought, Good Lord! She thought, *Darling,* and her color rose, and she went into the bathroom and stood under the shower and then went back to the bedroom again. She ran a comb through her hair, touched her happy mouth with lipstick and wrapped herself in the big robe. Then she pounded on Miles' door.

"Hey," he said, sleepily, "who is it?"

"Me," said Carol. "May I come in?"

"At your own risk," he replied, and his voice was no longer drowsy.

She went in and he was sitting up in bed, his hair at crazy angles, his thin face flushed with sleep. He reached for a pack of cigarettes on the bedside table and she said severely, "You shouldn't, before breakfast."

He put the pack down. "Come here," he ordered and she came and sat on the edge of the bed.

"Kiss me," he asked, "for good morning?"

She kissed his cheek, and the corner of his

mouth. She said, "Look, while I get breakfast, go take your swim. I don't think there'll be a human being around — and there's a robe of Adam's in the closet. How did you sleep?"

"Like the dead," he said, and a swift shadow passed across his eyes. He let her hand go, took a cigarette from the pack, and grinned with defiance. He said, "We aren't married yet. And besides, I hate reformers."

Carol rose and went to the door. She looked back. She said, "I slept too. I didn't expect I would."

"Neither did I," said Miles, "and now will you get out of here? You may as well learn once and for all that I sleep raw but wouldn't you rather I just *told* you about it?"

She fled, laughing, back to her room and dressed — slacks again, a sweater, play shoes. She heard Miles go out on the side porch upon which his room opened. She saw him walking down the path, tall and free, Adam's big robe wrapped about him, his feet bare, a towel slung over his arm. He stepped on a stone and cursed freely in the bright sunshine.

When he returned coffee was ready and the eggs were frying. He came galloping into the kitchen, his hair sleek with water, his face shining with it, his feet making large wet prints on the floor.

Carol said, "For heaven's sake, go get dry, and we'll have breakfast on the porch."

She set the table and carried out the trays. When he appeared, shaven, brushed, in shirt and slacks, she was ready. She said, "Sorry, no bacon, but I nipped a piece of Mr. Griffin's special ham and fried it for you. And made biscuits."

He said reverently, "Would you be so good as to marry me, sometime before noon?"

That was a very wonderful day. Sun and sand, talk and silences. Adam's trunks were a little precarious but Carol found two very precious, formidable safety pins. She found, also, a forgotten bottle of sun tan oil with which she anointed Miles' back. He had gained weight during his leave but he was still too thin, she thought, stroking the oil on gently, marking the fine, smooth skin, the good muscles, and too prominent ribs.

They swam, and dried in the sun. They lay on an old blanket and ate sandwiches and drank iced tea. And after that, while they were talking Miles fell asleep. Carol sat beside him a long time, shielding his face from the sun, watching it, so vulnerable in sleep and heartbreakingly young.

When he woke he would not believe that he had slept. They went in for another swim and then up to the shed and between them carried the light boat to the bank, pushed and pulled it down, hauled it to the water's edge and launched it. It leaked, but not very much. Miles went and got the oars and they rowed out on the bright, quiet breast of the water and sat there looking at the bank and the pines and the brown, weathered house. He said, after a moment, "I wish we could come here after we are married. We could, perhaps."

She said, "I haven't changed my mind."

"Exasperating," he said. "I hope the boat leaks furiously and that we sink. I won't lift a hand to save you, darling."

She said, serenely, "I swim fairly well."

"Don't I know it," he said gloomily. "No dice — and I'm cold. Let's get back. Wonder if we could catch some fish — got any bait?"

"Worms," she answered, "if you want to dig 'em. And there are old sweaters of Father's around somewhere."

He said, "Well, let's get going. Fish for supper."

That was how Dudley Lennox found them, an hour later, just at sunset, Miles digging worms with a trowel, and cursing happily when he unearthed one, while Carol,

212

sitting on a log beside him, looked over the fishing tackle.

When Dudley drove in, Carol's accustomed ear recognized the familiar stutter of the Griffin Ford. She grinned at Miles. "When you didn't show up last night," she said, "Mr. G. could no longer contain himself. He's probably brought me fresh supplies . . ."

He had also brought her ex-fiancé.

Dudley hopped briskly out of the car. He said, cordially, "Hello you two — you look very domestic. I come, bearing messages, and stuff."

"And at a very opportune time," added Carol brightly.

Mr. Griffin looked a little dazed. He said, "I brought you some things, Carol — thought you might run out, with company."

Dudley walked over to the log and looked down at Carol. Miles, looking rather absurd with a large earthworm in his hand, had risen. And Dudley asked, pleasantly, "Do you think you could give me supper, Carol? I've arranged for Mr. Griffin to come back and take me to the evening train."

"Oh, must you?" asked Carol. "Miles is driving back in the morning. You can get a train from the Field."

Dudley shook his head. He said, "Too

sorry, but I have to be in the office tomorrow and then take the noon train to Washington." He watched Mr. Griffin carrying the packages into the house. He added, "Sure you don't mind my staying for supper?"

"We'd love it," said Miles with such idiotic exaggeration that Carol began to laugh, helplessly. She fell off the log and Dudley picked her up and put her on her feet. Mr. Griffin emerged from the house and regarded the group with consternation. He didn't know what it was all about and he hoped Carol wouldn't give him fits for bringing Lennox out. But he couldn't refuse. He'd walked into the store, bold as brass, and said, "I have an important message for Miss Hillary. I understand she's at her place near here. Could you possibly drive me out?"

It was all too much for poor Mr. G. — former fiancé turning up, cool as cucumbers, to say nothing of Fighter Pilots who dropped in to spend the night. Minnie would be out of her romantic mind with curiosity. He wished he hadn't told her that the young man would be coming back to spend the night with them. She'd put on the best bolster cover and the embroidered pillow slips for her spare room.

He said, "Well, I'll go along now, Carol. Be back for you, Mr. Lennox, in time for the train."

The Ford rattled off. A slight constraint fell and the sunset wind was chilly. Carol said, after a moment, "We were going fishing."

"So I deduced. Don't let me interrupt you."

"You are, and have," she said, with anger. Then she laughed. She said, "This is a silly situation. Miles, release that worm. You look absurd. Let's all go into the house."

When they went in Dudley looked around him. He said, "I like this place — does it have a bar?"

"Nope," said Carol, "it's as dry as PX. Soft drinks only. What's the message, Dudley?"

"It's from your mother," he said.

"Sit down," said Carol, "and shoot."

He looked a little as if he'd like to, literally, and Miles grinned. But he wasn't particularly enjoying the situation. The average man is conventional at heart — except when he can get away with unconventionality.

Dudley said, sitting down, "It's a longish story. I ran into your mother in Washington. She was doing a lecture, and we had supper together, afterward."

"How nice," said Carol politely. She could

imagine that supper, she thought, with some bitterness.

Dudley said, "I told her that I was, upon returning home, going down to Southampton." He smiled at Carol. "Do you remember our story on ex-Senator Sniffen?" he asked, and when she nodded, he added, "Well, he wants to sue."

"Good Lord," said Carol, "I didn't know."

"You've been out of touch," he said mildly. He glanced at Miles. "I went down, spent the night at his place and persuaded him to reconsider. Not that we mind suits, we usually win 'em," he added casually, "but in this case there were several factors involved, most of them political — and tied up with the coming elections. We needn't go into that. The point is that I told Helen that I'd be on the Island and she suggested that I drop by. I got a lift this far. I'm to tell you that she's coming down for the weekend. Her present trip ends in Philadelphia on Thursday and she'll be down Friday. She wants you to get some local domestic help — she's bringing one of her secretaries, I think — and expects to finish the book. In passing, I may say, I've had a stroke of luck. I saw the manuscript and persuaded her to let us have it. She had, you know, refused several magazine offers.

But if it is in our hands by next week we can rush it through and she won't lose any time, nor, I may add ruefully, any money."

"That's fine," said Carol.

Miles said, "If you'll excuse me I think I'll put on some clothes. This sweater has been attacked by moths and bazookas."

He disappeared, and Dudley looked at Carol. He said, "You appear more at ease than the boy friend."

"Naturally," she said serenely, "as he is more conventional than I."

He said thoughtfully, "I told your mother I thought you were in love with him. She was appalled."

"That's interesting," said Carol, "and how did you arrive at that conclusion?"

"Well," he answered, "you told me there was someone else. I was very stupid about it. Then I thought things over, put two and two together . . ." He looked at her. He asked, "Just where do you expect this sort of — interlude will get you?"

"I haven't looked ahead," Carol answered, "and wherever it goes is none of your business."

"Roger," he agreed, "now that you speak the language of the air force. Still you can't expect me not to feel concerned."

He looked more than concerned; he

looked savagely angry. Yet he kept his voice down, occasionally he smiled. Carol didn't like his smile nor anything about him. She said, "If you intend to tell my family that Miles and I spent last night here —"

He said, nastily, "Wouldn't you consider it my duty?"

"Oh sure," said Carol, "also your good deed for the day. But don't struggle with your conscience, as I have every intention of telling them myself — and had before you arrived in the picture."

He said, "Funny thing. I thought he might be here. I called him at the Field, from Southampton. I'd been talking to the office and word had come through that Lt. Colonel Renshaw is missing. I knew he was a friend of Duncan's, and I thought I'd tell him before it was released for publication. At the Field they told me he was away for a couple of days. I called the house to make sure you were in the country and spoke to Aunt Agatha. When the Senator's friends dropped me in the village at Mr. Griffin's, I asked him — one of my hunches," he added modestly, "if you had guests. He said, yes, one. But even so," he added, "I was somewhat astonished when we drove in."

Miles spoke from the doorway. He said, "Very naturally." He looked at Carol. He stood very straight and tall, back in uniform. He said, "I believe the phrase is, we want you to be the first to know . . ."

"Miles," said Carol, "please . . ."

"Well," said Miles irritatingly, "it's too bad, old man, but the best man won and all that. Carol and I are going to be married. And now would you rather congratulate us and stay to supper, or shall I knock you down and sit on you till Mr. Griffin calls for the remains?"

Carol said, sharply, "Miles, don't be an utter idiot."

He lounged into the room. He said, "Perhaps I'm just a country boy. But there is something in Mr. Lennox's tone that I didn't like — much."

Dudley said, "This isn't a theater of war, Major, and there is no need for heroics. You can't expect me to be particularly happy over your announcement. You see, for some time I believed that Carol would marry me. And I still believe it."

Carol said, a little wildly, "I haven't said I'm going to marry anyone!"

Dudley raised his eyebrows. He asked, "Aren't you being a little premature, Duncan?"

"Hell, no!" said Miles.

Carol got to her feet. She said, resignedly,

"Well, fight it out, you two. I'm going to start supper and I hope every mouthful chokes you both."

She went into the kitchen very rapidly and slammed the door. She stood there a moment, thinking. She was furious with Dudley Lennox, she was furious with Miles. If he had thought he had to — if he thought *that,* he could go fly a kite and she would die an old maid. She felt the tears slide down her cheeks and she brushed them away angrily. She wasn't marrying Miles Duncan because a man with whom she had thought herself in love came galloping up in a Ford out of the blue, took one look at the situation and jumped to a conclusion. She grinned, shakily. He hadn't far to jump, she thought, so how could she blame him.

In the living room Miles stood by the fireplace. He said, "I asked Carol to marry me last night."

"And?" asked Lennox quietly.

"And," said Miles, "she answered that we would wait for a time — until my next orders, for instance — and then talk it over."

"She's never," murmured Lennox, "been very sure of herself. I asked her for six straight months before she said yes. And *that* didn't stick. I suppose she thinks she's in love with you."

"Evidently," said Miles.

"She thought," said Dudley, "that she was in love with me." He got up from the chair in which he had sat, unstirring, for the last few minutes. He said, "I admire you, Duncan, and I envy you. I admire your crazy courage and I envy you your opportunity to display it. I envy you your youth, I don't especially like you, any more than you like me, but I respect you. And as far as Carol is concerned, you have my blessing, for as long as it lasts. For, I think she'll get over you, and come back to me. If I didn't believe that I'd *let* you knock me down. You can, you know. You're considerably taller, you have a longer reach and you're in better condition. But I'll take my chances on surviving. However, I see no special need for dramatics at the moment. Because whether you marry or not — I'm still in the running."

Miles was white. He said, "That's fine."

Lennox smiled. He said, "Don't distress yourself, Major. And I don't know how much you overheard of my conversation with Carol. I don't think you heard that your friend, Lt. Colonel Renshaw, is missing."

Miles took a step forward and sat down abruptly. He said, "Pete . . . missing . . . ?"

"Yes," said Dudley. "It hasn't been made

public as yet. His family has just been notified. I remembered that, in the various in-
terviews you gave after your return, his name
was frequently mentioned — as one of your
close friends."

"My closest," said Miles dully. "He was
due for a leave pretty soon. His wife lives in
Great Neck. I've seen her since my return."
He put his hand over his face, his gesture
uncertain. When he took it away again his
face was suffused with blood. "God damn
them!" he said.

Lennox rose. He said, "I'm sorry, Duncan."

"*You're sorry!*" said Miles. "Well, thanks
for telling me." He got up and went into the
kitchen. He said, "Carol — ?"

She turned, and looked at him and went
swiftly into his arms. She didn't care that
Dudley had followed, that he stood there at
the open door and saw.

"What is it, darling?" she asked.

"It's Pete," he told her. "Pete Renshaw . . .
Lennox says he's missing. I've got to see his
wife. She hasn't anybody here in the East —
she came East with the kid, thinking he'd be
here on leave soon — she's been living in
South Dakota."

She said, practically, "Of course you must
go, Miles. But you can wait long enough to

have something to eat."

"I don't want anything," he said angrily.

She said, "You must, dear. If only coffee . . . and then you can drive there, tonight. You can stop and 'phone, in the village."

Dudley said, "You can give me a lift, Duncan."

Carol drew away from Miles. She said, "I don't think so, Dudley. I think you'd better take the train."

She looked from one to the other. She said, "I'll get supper ready at once. You can both help."

They ate in the kitchen. Carol made strong coffee, a salad, sliced the ham and fried potatoes. She said, once, "It isn't a varied diet," and Dudley said, "I never believed in vitamins anyway." There was little general conversation. Miles ate sparingly and with an effort but drank several cups of coffee. Toward the end of the meal he set down his cup, looked at Carol, and spoke to her as if they were alone. He said:

"I'm sorry you didn't know Pete. He's one of the best. He's a big guy — we used to kid him because his hair curled and he looked like one of these movie heroes. He got married before he went overseas — he's never seen his kid. I looked up his wife when I first came to New York and she's been over to the Field. Her name's Ruth. She's about your size, Carol, and cute."

He was silent. Dudley looked at Carol but she was sitting quietly at the table, watching Miles. He saw the intentness, the gravity, the concentration of her regard, and for the first time felt actual fear lest he had, in truth, lost her.

Miles said, conversationally, as if he and Carol had been arguing, "You see how it is, darling? Pete always talked about what he and Ruth would do when he got back. He had the kid entered at his old prep school. He said, 'We'll make a football player of him.' "

Carol said, "Missing isn't dead. But if he is, they were married. And she has the baby."

He looked at her. Dudley Lennox felt an enormous, unusual embarrassment. He had no right to be here. It was indecent. He could rise and go quietly away and they would not know it. Yet he could not move. He was as if paralyzed. He had to hear and see this for himself.

Miles asked, "You think that would be compensation? Hell, you didn't know Pete and how they felt about each other."

She said, "I know how I feel about you.

Of course, it isn't compensation. But it's something."

He said, as if he hadn't heard, "I used to watch Pete in the Ready Room — he'd sit and listen, his hands back of his head and a goofy grin on his face. The rest of us would sweat under the collar and spit cotton, but not Pete. He was nuts about flying. He was the best Goddamned flyer I ever knew. He used to sing — a lot. Drove us crazy. He had a good voice. He'd sing — you know how it goes . . ." He hummed it, spoke the words . . . " 'Old pilots never fly, they only draw their pay . . .' " His voice broke, he stood up and shoved back his chair. "Guess I'd better go," he said.

Carol said, "Let's get your things together."

They walked out of the kitchen. Dudley sat still, lit a cigarette. He thought, If it's like that? His strong jaw was set, hard. He thought, If they aren't married before he leaves, there's a chance. He thought of Helen. She was an ally. Adam, he told himself, wouldn't be.

Carol watched Miles fling his few belongings in the little bag. She said, "Here are your brushes," and held them out to him. He took them, put them in. Then he took her by the shoulders. He said, "This isn't the way we meant things to be."

"No."

"Are you staying on here?"

She said, "For a few days. Mother's coming — she expects me to stay."

He said, "I'll write. Can you get to Griffin's and call me at the Field?"

"I'll call."

"You'll come up to town?" he asked.

"As soon as I can. Miles?"

"Yes?"

She said, "How much of what you said to Dudley was cover-up for the situation?"

He smiled, for the first time since he had learned about Renshaw. He said, "None. He didn't have a shotgun, did he?"

She said, quietly, "You must be sure . . ."

He said, as if he hadn't heard her, "There's always the chance that he bailed out. But the worst of it is hoping — and keeping on hoping. But what else can I tell her to do?"

"Nothing," she said, thickly, "nothing."

"Well," he said, "I'd better get under way . . ." He put his arm around her, kissed her hard, and quickly. He said, "If you want me to take Lennox along . . . ?"

"No. Mr. Griffin will be up presently," she said. She tried to laugh, failed, "Dudley can help wash the dishes. Don't worry."

He said, "Well, I'd rather be alone . . ."

He walked out ahead of her, his bag in his hand, his cap on the side of his head. Dudley was waiting in the living room. He asked, as they entered, "Sure you don't want me along, Duncan? I can drive, I know the way."

"Thanks," said Miles, "I'll manage."

At the car he bent to kiss Carol. He said, "I'll see you later," and climbed in. The engine started, the car went off down the road, swaying, jouncing. They stood and watched it in the darkness, until they no longer saw the tail light.

Carol said, "I have to wash up."

They went back to the kitchen and Dudley watched her moving about, running hot water in the sink, washing the dishes and glasses, scraping pans. He sat, and smoked and made no move to help her. Let her do it herself, and forget that he was there, if she wished. He said, after a while:

"Sorry I had to break in like this."

She said, "You're not sorry, really."

"I suppose not. Are you going to marry him?"

"Yes."

"When?"

She moved her shoulders impatiently, "How do I know?" she said.

He said, "You won't listen but you're making a mistake. He's just a kid. You're much more mature. His maturity has been forced upon him by the conditions of war and combat. Like most youngsters in his situation, he's grown up too fast in one way; in another, it's arrested development. It won't be flags flying and medals. The flags will be furled, the medals will rattle around in a tin box. You have to think of that, and of adjustments, when he comes back. Hard adjustments. We are beginning to see them already. These kids miss the excitement and the total abnormality of their lives. They won't be able to settle down. What has he to offer you as a civilian?"

She said, "We love each other."

"Is that enough?"

"It's enough for me." She looked at him, her eyes dark with anger. She said, "Okay — granted I treated you badly, granted I'm a heel — wouldn't I have been more of a heel if I'd gone through with it knowing I didn't love you? Granted the whole business, still, what right have you to interfere?"

He said, "I love you, Carol, and a damned sight more adequately than a youngster in hero's livery who comes back from God knows where, drooling over the first good looking white woman he's seen in months and when that's no dice — because your mother has plenty of hard, common sense —

switching his affections to her daughter —"

Carol's hand closed over the cup she was putting away. She lifted her hand. The cup sailed over his head as he ducked, and crashed against the wall. The act of small violence released the tension in her and she began to cry, hard, wrenching sobs. She said, incoherently as he rose and came toward her, "Don't — don't *touch* me!"

She ran out of the kitchen and he heard a door slam. After a moment he lit a cigarette and stood at the door waiting for Griffin. He thought, I hope he remembered I left my bag in his store; he thought, I wish to God he'd hurry.

After what seemed like a long time he heard the Ford rattling along the road. He went through the living room to the bedrooms and knocked on the first closed door. He said, "I'm going now, Carol."

She did not answer but he could hear her moving about the room.

He went out and called Griffin. He said, "I'm ready."

On Friday Mr. Griffin met the train and brought Helen Hillary and the efficient Miss Goddard to the cottage. Helen, in a black linen suit with a blouse the color of young leaves, looked, he told her, as well as he'd ever seen her. She said that he did, too, and how was Minnie and had he heard from the boy? They talked of weather, of war and then of Carol. Helen said, "I thought she'd walk down and meet us."

He hadn't seen her, said Griffin, since yesterday. Jessie was up to the cottage and everything was in order.

She asked carelessly, "Was Mr. Lennox here?"

"Yep," said Griffin, "he come by car, and then I took him out and called for him that evening."

He volunteered no further information. Helen, with a mental shrug, called Miss Goddard's attention to the beauties of nature along the way.

They found Jessie in the kitchen, getting their late luncheon ready. Carol, she reported, was out fishing. Helen, standing on the porch, could see her half way across the bay, anchored, a small lonely figure in the rowboat.

Miss Goddard unpacked. She set up her typewriter and put out her notebooks, and the manuscript. She had the tools of her trade assembled in the living room when Helen decided that they could work better on the porch. Miss Goddard reassembled. Helen came out of her bedroom, which

Carol had vacated and Jessie re-made, and wandered through the house. It was, she thought, a charming place. Her first enthusiasm for it had, of course, passed but she still liked it. Pausing in the room which had been Miles', she went to the windows and looked out. She noticed a moment later, a cigarette burn on the sill, and frowned. This was the room Adam often occupied. It was like him to leave burning cigarettes around. A crooked rag rug annoyed her and she stooped to straighten it. From beneath it she picked up a paper match cover, and looked at the printing on it idly — Officers Club.

She stood with it in her hand. Carol could have dropped it. But to the best of Helen's knowledge Miles had not been in town since he had been ordered to the Long Island field. Nor did she believe that Carol knew any other officer stationed there.

Still, she might have obtained it anywhere, Helen thought, at the house of a friend, for instance.

She put the matches in her pocket, went out and down to the beach. Carol was rowing in, and Helen waved to her. She sat down on a log and watched the boat grow larger, and the figure in it. Carol beached the boat, drew it up and Helen rose and came to meet her. She said, smiling, "How brown you've grown in a few days."

"Brown," agreed Carol, "and freckled." She was, her mother saw, noticeably thinner.

Helen said, "Washington was as usual. I suppose Dudley told you he saw me there? Mr. Griffin said that he'd stopped in."

"Yes," said Carol, "he was here for a little while."

Her mother said, "My trip was quite successful — I expect to go to the coast, later in the summer. Did Dudley tell you *Foresight* is taking the book, a shortened version, of course."

"Yes," Carol said.

Her mother looked at her as they went up the steps and on the porch. She commented, "You aren't very communicative." She put her hand in her pocket. "I found this in your father's room. I'm rather curious about it."

Carol looked at the matches. She said, "Miles must have dropped them."

"When was he here?" asked Helen.

Carol sat down on the long divan heaped with faded cushions and took a cigarette from her pocket. She used Miles' matches to light it, and kept them, in her hand. She said, "The other day. He came unexpectedly, in a car he'd borrowed. Mr. Griffin directed him. He stayed here that night and the next day. He was to remain another

232

night but Dudley came. He told Miles that a friend of his, a man named Renshaw, is missing."

"It's in the morning papers," said Helen evenly.

"It hadn't been released then," said Carol. "Miles went on to Great Neck to see Mrs. Renshaw. Dudley left on the train."

Her mother asked, "Was it quite wise of you to encourage gossip?"

She felt that she could not trust her voice, yet she managed to speak normally.

Carol looked at her, directly.

She said, "I doubt if the Griffins gossip but it doesn't matter whether they do or not. I expect you think that, if you hadn't found the matches —"

"Well?"

"I would have told you," said Carol. "Miles and I are going to be married. He asked me, the night he came. He wishes to be married as soon as possible. But I thought it best to wait a little —"

Helen said, with her most refrigerated inflection, "Which shows a little intelligence."

Carol said, quickly, "Miles believes that his next orders will take him south, or west, as an instructor, and he may be there some time before returning to combat. In that case, we could be married before he leaves, or I could follow him out and marry him there."

"You are aware that I entirely disapprove?"

"Of course," said Carol. She rose. "Sorry, but I'd better go wash up now. And also I must deliver the fish to Jessie, I left them on the steps," she said.

She went out, and Helen stood looking over the water. She thought, I'll see Dudley as soon as I return to town. Yet how could Lennox help her? There must be some way. Adam was out of the question. Miles himself?

Miles. It couldn't all be lost, the adoration and the wonder. He would listen to her, she would make him listen.

She told herself, looking with unseeing eyes at the blue water and the wooded land beyond, that she would *not* have this for Carol — the risk and uncertainty, the almost inevitable sorrow — or, at least, disillusionment. What did Carol or any of them know about this boy — save that he was charming and a hero? Carol was both stupid, and stubborn. She would exchange security and an ordered life for insecurity and disorder. Dudley could give her everything; Miles, nothing which endured.

She must talk to Miles and convince him.

Chapter Sixteen

Helen worked over the weekend, she worked most of each day and half of the night. Miss Goddard looked as if she had been drawn through a keyhole — Helen, as if she had slept happily and awakened refreshed, on the other side of it. Carol walked to the village every evening and telephoned Miles. Her mother did not ask her where she was going nor what she intended to do. She did not mention Miles again except to ask, "Are you announcing this — engagement?" and Carol answered, "No, I don't think it's necessary. There have been too many announcements already."

Miles had written her. He had spent the night at Mrs. Renshaw's and then returned to camp. He said, "I can't write you about it. It hit her where she lives. She was glad to see me. You see, no one here knows Pete. Talking to someone who does made a difference."

When Helen and Miss Goddard left, Carol went with them. In town she would feel closer to Miles, and he could get in to see her occasionally. She had her work at the hospital and she wished to talk to her father and Agatha.

She spoke to Adam first, invading his workroom on the evening she returned shortly after dinner. She sat opposite him, at his big desk. Miss Perdon departed, the room was quiet and warm with the sultry dregs of day. She told him about Miles, quietly, frankly.

He said, "If that's what you want, I'm for it. He's a good kid. He hasn't found himself yet, but he will. It will have to be the hard way — for all men like Miles."

She said, "Mother is definitely against it."

"She would be," said Adam. "But this is something which basically concerns only you and Miles. You'll have to make your own decisions and your own mistakes. You can take what comes, Carol. You're strong enough. You can stand on your own feet."

He rose, smiled at her, came around and put his hand on her shoulder. He said, "I remember our conversation not so long ago — at Henri's place, wasn't it? You asked me if just physical attraction was enough."

She said, "It isn't *just* —"

"So, you've found that out? Good."

She had found it out the first night at the cottage. She had rediscovered it the next morning, listening to Miles talk about Pete

Renshaw, wishing to take his hurt and shock and make it her own, feeling the immense compassion of a mother, the tenderness of a lover, knowing that when he looked at her, and she at him, there was no desire, only an unspoken sharing . . . knowing that he could not so look, nor so speak, if he did not love her . . . understanding that this heavy longing for identification with the beloved was, in its essence, of the spirit . . . the longing which expresses itself in touch and rapture, in physical union . . . the universal longing which, as a strong tree, is rooted in earth and from earth derives its nourishment, but reaches its aspiring arms upward, toward heaven.

She put her hand over her father's.

"I've found out . . ." she said.

Later, she told Agatha. Agatha listened, and said, after a while, "It won't be easy, Carol."

"I know that," Carol told her.

Agatha said, "I liked that boy from the moment I set eyes on him. But — not that you'll listen to me — you mustn't risk your future, rushing blindly into a war marriage."

"It isn't blindly."

"That's as may be," Agatha said. "Your mother hasn't been herself since you returned. You've told her?"

"Yes. She's very much opposed to the idea."

Agatha said, "I dare say." She looked around her room, in which they were sitting after their strained and silent family dinner. The champagne Adam produced had gone flat in the glasses. Miles hadn't been able to come up from the field. It had been, all in all, a rather dreadful little dinner. "But," ended Agatha, "it is after all, your business."

Two allies. Well, that was something. Not that it would matter if every hand in this house and in the world beyond were against them, thought Carol, going to her own room to write to Miles.

On an impulse, the next day, she went around to see Jenny Davis and found her having a noon breakfast in bed. It was not a matinee day and Jenny could indulge herself.

"Lunch?" asked Jenny. "Golly, I'm glad to see you, Carol. What's new?"

"No lunch," said Carol, "I've had mine." She plucked a bit of celery from the tray, nibbled it reflectively, and asked, "Were you surprised when I broke my engagement to Dudley?"

"Not especially."

"Would you be, if I told you I were going

to marry Miles Duncan?"

Jenny's eyes widened, and she moved suddenly to embrace Carol with the result that the tray all but slid to the floor. Carol retrieved bread and celery, radishes and raw carrots from the bedspread. "Hey," she said, "take it easy."

Jenny's eyes filled with her facile but genuine tears. She said, "I had a hunch the night I joined you at Henri's' and saw you dancing together."

"So did I," Carol said.

"When will you be married? Can I give you a party?"

Carol said, "We've had enough parties and we don't know when." She thought, I'm sure — but I have to know that he is. She added, "We aren't announcing it. I haven't told anyone except the family and you. Miles hasn't any family to tell." She added, "Dudley knows, too."

"I hope he took it badly," said Jenny. She asked, "What does your father think?"

"He's for it."

Jenny hesitated . . . "Helen . . . ?" she asked.

Carol shook her head. "She doesn't like it," she said.

Jenny said softly, "I'm sorry, for your sake." She leaned forward again and took Carol's hand. She said, "Hold on to happiness, Carol. It's hard to find and so difficult to keep . . ."

Helen's manuscript was in at the *Foresight* office. She took it there herself, to the mild astonishment of her agent. She put it on Dudley's desk. "I'm as good as my word," she said.

"Better." He smiled. "The check goes forward to Hanson's office today."

She said impatiently, "I don't care about that. I don't care about anything but Carol and this — this recent stupidity."

"How do you suppose I feel?" He leaned back and looked at her. "Have you seen him?" he asked.

"Last night. I was at the dinner for the Chinese generals. When I came home, he was leaving — I had no opportunity to talk with him. He and Adam, Carol and Aunt Agatha had had a cosy family dinner."

He asked, "How do they feel about it?"

"Wonderful," said Helen. "I could murder them." She looked at Dudley. She said, "I apologize for my child. She's treated you outrageously."

"Young love," he said, and smiled. He added, "I suppose Adam is delighted. He never liked me."

"He's like a shot in the arm to Carol," said

Helen. "He backs her up at every opportunity. If he weren't in the picture . . ."

They looked at one another. Dudley grinned. He said, "I think you've got something there — possibly it could be arranged."

Helen rose. She smiled, brilliantly. She said, "That's all I want to know."

On the following morning, Adam Hillary sat where Helen had sat, and looked across the same desk at Dudley Lennox. Dudley had been talking for some time. Now he was concluding and Adam listened quietly. Only his eyes and his gesture as he relit his cold pipe betrayed his excitement.

"And so," said Dudley, "as we are transferring Owens from the Pacific theater to the London office and pulling Davis out of London and bringing him back home — he hasn't been well, he rates a rest — there's a place for you, Hillary, if you care to take it."

Adam said, "I thought you suspected me of senility."

Dudley shrugged. He said, "I've changed my mind. Look at Parsons," he added, naming a veteran Chicago newspaper man, "he's pushing sixty and doing a better job than most of the younger men, and stands up under it, too. Things are getting hotter. Everyone is looking toward invasion. But the Pacific remains the canker spot. If you want this, you can have it."

"When do I go?"

Dudley said, "There'll be the usual red tape, clearances, inoculations, all that. But we'll get things under way, today. In fact, I've laid a few lines already — just in case." He hesitated. "You're sure you want this?" he asked.

"Damned sure."

Dudley said, "Okay, it's in the bag." He looked at Adam and smiled. He said, "I'm feeling rather magnanimous. You've never liked me and I think you encouraged Carol in her — shall we call it, break for freedom?"

Adam said, "That's quite right. I didn't think you'd make a go of it."

"And you think she will with Duncan?"

Adam said, "I hope so, but I don't know. How the hell does anyone know?"

Dudley said, carefully, "I should remind you that you're leaving her in something of a spot. When I talked to Helen recently, she was exceedingly upset by the proposed alliance."

Adam said, "Carol's not in any spot. She's free, white and over twenty-one. She can do as she pleases. As a matter of fact, it won't hurt her if I clear out. She'll learn to stand alone, as for the most part, she's been compelled to do." He added, "And another thing, I want this job for a number of reasons. I want to take a look at things for myself, and also to find a clearer personal perspective. There's a conclusion, or two, I think I might arrive at, if I get away from here — from everybody."

"If you have time," said Dudley, "to arrive at any conclusions."

Miles came up from the Field. He was tired, the last few days had been crowded. He hadn't seen Carol in nearly a week and summer was thick and dusty on the city streets. He rode with the taxi top open and tried to find some decent air to breathe. He hadn't been able to get Renshaw out of his mind. He dreamed about him. He dreamed of Renshaw's wife sitting, that night, in the small living room of the rented house, her face like nothing on earth, her distended eyes dry. She had gone from the room once and brought the sleeping baby in; she had put the child in Miles' arms and said, "Pete never saw him. He looks like Pete, doesn't he? Do you suppose I'm imagining it? Do you suppose he'll grow up still looking like him?"

The cab stopped at the Hillary house, he

went up the steps and Ole let him in. Ole said, "Mrs. Hillary is in the drawing room, Major."

Miles went in. Helen was sitting there, alone. It was not quite dark. The room was filled with a rosy, dusty light. She rose and gave him both her hands. She said, smiling, "You'll have to bear with me for a little while, Miles. Carol had to go out."

Very fortuitously, she thought. She went on, and motioned him to sit opposite her. "An unfortunate thing happened, today. One of the girls in her office, to whom she had become attached, has had word that her husband was killed on a training flight. She tried to kill herself. Dreadful," said Helen, "and so unnecessary, poor child. Carol is still on vacation, but the girl's sister 'phoned her — she thought Carol might have some influence. So Carol went over to Brooklyn. She wasn't taken to the hospital. She didn't know much about drugs, and she took too much. It just made her ill —"

Miles said, "That's a hell of a thing for Carol to have to go through."

"Yes," said Helen. She added, "Has Carol told you about her father?"

"That he's going overseas for *Foresight*? Sure," said Miles, "she told me."

Helen said, "Curious, how so much has

happened in a short time — our meeting for instance —" She paused, gave him time to remember, and was gratified to see him redden, slightly — "and then, coming home — Carol's engagement to Dudley and after that —" She moved her shoulders a little — "her engagement to you."

He said, soberly, "I hope you understand." He looked at her and smiled. And she thought, with a sudden, savage anger, Why did Carol have to do this? I have so little, I ask so little! There are a thousand bright young men in the world, she could meet and love any of them.

She had kept the fiction carefully uppermost in her mind; the fiction that her opposition to this marriage was for Carol's sake. But she was perfectly aware that it was fiction. She was equally conscious that her dominating emotion was envy — not because of Miles, himself, but because of all he stood for, youth, ardor, happiness. These things she envied her daughter with a despair and savagery which she had not felt in many years. She had not wanted Miles as her lover, nor as her friend, nor yet, as she had often said, to take the place of the son she had never wished nor had. She had wanted him as a symbol, as a sign. As reassurance — the reassurance that she was still desirable, still lovely, still able to stir the strong, blind emotions. With the boy himself she was not concerned; he was nothing to her as a person, and had never been.

She asked gently, "Do you love Carol?"

"Yes," he said, and his face lighted. "I love her more than I thought I'd ever love anyone. It — keeps growing. I —" he leaned forward, disarmed, sure of her concern, her generosity and her affection for them both. He said, "Persuade her to marry me, Helen, at once."

She touched his hand with her own, and leaned back in her chair. She said, "There's no one I'd rather see her marry — if the circumstances were different. You know that. You know how fond I am of you. But, Carol's happiness comes first. Somehow, I can't believe this is for her happiness. She hasn't the remotest idea of what it may mean. It's — oh, you *must* see this, Miles — glamour, war, all the rest of it. I can't bear to have her made unhappy," she told him, her voice darkly lovely with sorrow and apprehension. "Yet I have nothing to say, she is of age, she can do as she pleases, and as I have told you, she listens to her father rather than to me. I haven't drawn an easy breath since I first suspected how things were. Miles, you must make her listen to you — you must convince her you wish to wait until after the war. For her sake. If you love her you will do this, that is, if you love her unselfishly. I know her better than you. She couldn't take it, she is neither mature nor strong enough. And there is no one who can persuade her except you. Believe me," she said earnestly, "if you marry now, and if something happens — and it does happen," she reminded him — "even in a routine flight —"

He said, "She's willing to take that chance."

"Are you?" asked Helen. She looked at him and played an ace. She said, "I understand that you were very close to the flyer who was just recently reported missing. Carol told me that you went at once to see his wife. Can you think of Carol in her place?"

His face changed and hardened. He said, "I have thought of her."

"Yet you can risk putting her through that?" asked Helen. She paused a moment. There was one card more. She asked, quietly, her face grave and concerned, "Or is it because of your — unexpected visit to the cottage, Miles, that you feel you and Carol must undertake a hasty and immediate marriage?"

Chapter Seventeen

Helen waited, watching Miles, for the angry denial. To her complete astonishment, it did not come quite soon enough. There was a perceptible hiatus between her question and his answer. He said, his face suffused with hot, sudden blood, "What a damnable thing to ask! Of course not —"

She was not persuaded. She had asked the question as an adept player plays a card. Her reasoning, like herself, was devious. She had thought, If anything will convince him of the folly of a hasty marriage, it's the implication that I — or anyone else — might believe it necessary — or, at least, indicated. She had not for a moment believed that Miles and Carol, playing at love in a cottage, had been anything but idiotic and innocent. If the question had been put to her she would have repudiated it with laughter. How absurd, she knew Carol too well!

Did she? What woman knows her own daughter? She thought, *But it isn't possible!* Yet anything was possible, she reminded herself. Carol was Adam's child. She did not remind herself, as well, Carol is *my* child.

Her question had been a matter of technique. But now, she stared at Miles with horror and a curious pervasive hatred, which had nothing to do with morals or maternal anxiety.

She said, coldly, "You do not convince me!"

Miles' color was normal again. He ran his hand over his head in a restless, abstracted gesture and his carefully brushed hair stood, literally, on end. He looked very young and troubled.

It had been a damnable thing to ask, because it might have been true. He had remembered, between question and answer, the firelight in the cottage, and another urgent question. "Carol?" he had asked, and she had said, regarding him with her luminous eyes, her mouth vulnerable from kissing, "No, darling —"

She had been wise for them both and it was remembering her wisdom which had retarded his answer, which had brought the blood to his face and accelerated his pulse.

He said, desperately, "You must believe me, Helen."

"Why?" she inquired, "on what basis? I don't know you very well, Miles. I don't know what you were before you put on a uniform, nor whether a uniform has released your inhibitions. Nor, in fact, whether or not you had any to release."

He said, after a moment, "Very well. So you don't know me. But you do know Carol."

"As to that," she murmured, "I cannot say. I thought I did —"

She permitted her voice to trail off, as if it had been wounded, as if it bled.

He asked, harshly, "Do you intend to cross-examine Carol?"

"What would you do," she inquired, "if you were in my place?"

He didn't know. He was not Carol's mother.

She said, thoughtfully, before he could reply, "Or if you were Adam?"

He found himself shouting, careless whether Ole were within hearing, or Agatha or even Adam himself.

"You are going to suggest — ?"

She interrupted swiftly, and said smoothly, "He's her father, after all."

Sure. Put yourself in Adam's place. But you couldn't There was nothing paternal about your feelings for Carol Hillary. But if you and Carol were twenty odd years older, if you and Carol had a daughter . . . ?

He said, "There is no reason why we should hasten our marriage." He said it flatly, without inflection.

Helen said, presently, "In that case, there is no reason, either, why you should not convince Carol that it would be wiser to wait until after the war."

"All right," Miles said. They had made a bargain, and he knew it. She had said tacitly, call off this absurd idea of marrying at once and I'll say nothing either to Carol or her father.

Helen smiled, brilliantly. She reached out her hand and pulled the bell cord by the fireplace. She said, gently, "I think Ole must have cocktails ready. Agatha should be down by now, and Carol will surely be coming soon. I don't know about Adam, of course. He seems to be tearing all over town trying to expedite his departure. So silly of him," she added, shrugging, "at his age."

Ole appeared before there was any need for comment. The Martinis came with him and Miles drank two, in rapid succession, and with concentration of purpose. If ever a man needed a drink . . .

He could not remain angry with Helen Hillary. He was forced to take her at her face value, and her face was precious and treasurable. Not so long ago he had been in love with her, after a fashion. Oh, not in love, but near enough. She had given him gifts which he had forgotten existed — laughter, beauty, and that quality with a jaded name, glamour. She had given him gentleness, wit, and, he believed, understanding. He could not as quickly and readily reverse his conception of her. Returned to a more normal mode of living, a way of life which did not include death at any moment and from any quarter, the clear outline of her magic had dimmed, and the remembered excitement she had aroused in him had become embarrassed, had made him feel that he had been momentarily adolescent. She was not for him; and he had known it before he fell in love with Carol. Falling in love with Carol had been a completely absorbing experience — all emotion narrowed down to a fine burning point, fiercely concentrated and yet so encompassing that there was no room for anything else.

There was, moreover, no way in which he could know that Helen was not exactly as she seemed at this moment, precisely as she deliberately presented herself to him — a comprehensibly anxious mother, concerned only with the welfare, present and future, of her child.

A woman has, let us say, eight intimates — a husband, a lover, an enemy, a child, friends — and each of them sees her as a totally, or almost dissimilar person. Therefore, she is eight women. Also, she is a ninth woman, the woman she herself sees — and knows, in part, or whole. Miles saw Helen Hillary through his own eyes. He had no knowledge of her as a jealous, an envious woman, a woman who considered herself frustrated, or wronged, or slighted. He had no yardstick by which to measure her save that of his personal experience of her.

He set down his glass. He said, "Helen, if you would listen to me —"

"Oh hush," she said, and smiled for the first time. "We will say no more about it." She put her hand on his arm, decided that was a mistake, and withdrew it, but not too hastily.

They heard Agatha on the stairs. Her entrance was a diversion which both welcomed. She came in and greeted them, asked anxiously, "Has Carol returned yet?' and shook her head when they said, No, she had not. She took her tomato juice from the tray Ole offered and said, "She'll be terribly upset, poor child."

The conversation became general. Miles nursed his third cocktail and tried not to think — what would he say to her, how account for his reversal of opinion? Hell, he didn't know. He kept listening for her with his heart, and when, finally, the door opened and she came in, his heart turned over.

She looked as if she had been witnessing an execution. She was very pale, her linen suit was crumpled, the broad-brimmed hat she carried in her hand was as crushed as if she had sat on it. She tossed it, and her handbag, to a chair and Miles saw that the shadows under her eyes were dark and the eyes themselves faintly reddened. She had forgotten to replenish her lipstick, a smudge of dust was on one cheek. She looked plainer than he had ever seen her and he had never loved her as much.

Her tired regard surveyed them. She said, "Hello, everybody," and her small face was briefly illuminated as she looked at Miles. He had risen, and now took her hands in his, and was kissing her before them all, not caring. He said, "You poor kid."

Carol sat down, in the nearest chair. She said, "I could do with a drink — if there's time. I'll have to wash up."

"Of course, there's time," said Helen promptly and Ole, looking as concerned as his features permitted, passed the cocktail tray. Carol's hand shook slightly as she lifted the glass to her lips. And Helen said sympathetically, "It was pretty bad, wasn't it?"

"It was horrible," said Carol briefly. She looked at Miles and smiled. "Have you been waiting long, darling?" she asked, quite as if they were alone.

He was sanity, in a world which was insane. She thought, if she lived for a thousand years, she would not forget that crazy, paper-white girl in the narrow bed, in the hot, smothering room. "Why wouldn't they let me die?" she had kept asking. "There isn't any use going on. Not for me, there isn't."

A hasty marriage, a few weeks of happiness. Over now. She had told Carol about it, this afternoon. Long incoherent sentences, silences, tears. But the picture emerged, clear.

Just another girl with a job which paid thirty a week, living with her sister and brother-in-law and their two noisy kids in a flat too small for them. Never caring much about working, because she wanted, most of all, her own man and her own home. A place of her own, in which she was free to sing and laugh, to breathe and love. Marking time until then; doing her job as well as she could but not making it a goal. Carol, listening, had thought that, after all, the authentically ambitious woman is a sport of nature. This girl was almost any girl. Circumstances alter, environment, heredity — but basically most girls are alike — they are marking time.

This one was twenty. She had worked since she left school, at seventeen. Then she had met the boy she'd married. They'd had a weekend for a honeymoon and they'd lived in his parents' old brownstone house until it was time for him to go. When he was through with his primary and basic training and shifted to an advanced school, she'd expected to join him. A Cadet's wife, like so many others. She'd find a place to live, wherever he was, and she'd work in a store or some place until he graduated. After that, they could be together again for a little while.

But he had not finished his basic. Instead, his basic had finished him. Still she had tried to join him. God knows she had tried.

Carol put out her hand to Miles. She thought, I'll tell him, tonight. We can be married as soon as we have had the tests taken and can get the license.

She set down her glass and rose. "I'll be gone only a minute," she said.

During that minute, Adam came in. He looked heat-wilted but he was very happy. Things had gone well all day. He had seen Dudley, he reported, stretching his long legs, and accepting a drink, and everything was in order. It wouldn't be long now. He raised his glass to Miles. He said, "Two heroes in the family, perhaps," and then glanced at Helen with mock apology. "I was forgetting," he said courteously, "two heroes and one heroine."

But such luck as hers never ran his way. He wouldn't be torpedoed or if he were he'd never live to lecture about it. Any plane in which he flew would carry him safely to his destination. The bombs would not fall too near nor the shells. His personal adventures had ended with the last war, he thought, the cocktail glass smooth and round in his hand. Since then, or, since Europe after the war, perhaps, his adventures had all been vicarious and well compensated. He looked at Helen. What a fool she must think him, giving up the book, giving up the comfort he had become accustomed to, giving up ease and flattery.

And what else?

This was not his house, although he underwrote half of the expense. This was not his wife and had not been for many years. And although this was his daughter coming back into the room, her little face clean, and her lipstick valiant, she did not belong to him. She belonged to herself, and, if to anyone else, to the boy sitting there silent, abstracted, frowning a little, his hair badly in need of brushing and his uniform looking a little weary around the edges.

Which was as it should be.

But there was one person who belonged to him, as much as any adult can belong to another. She had said so this afternoon, when they had made their plans. Adam looked at Carol and was grateful to her. For there was no longer the slightest need of pretense. Carol had her own life to live and his would not concern her. As for Helen's old threat, "If you insist upon a divorce, I'll name Jenny Davis!" that no longer mattered. Jenny was not now concerned with a career. At the close of the play she would tour the camps and when the need for camp entertainment was over, she would retire from the stage. She had said today, "And I don't care what she does or says, Adam."

Before he left he would tell Helen that.

Ole announced dinner. Carol put her hand on Miles' arm. She said, wanly, "I never felt less like eating but I suppose we have to make the gesture."

After dinner, Agatha went to her room, Adam to his study and Helen upstairs to make some calls on her private wire. She reached Dudley Lennox at his home and talked to him for some time. When she was finished she replaced the telephone gently in its cradle. She called Cresson, to brush her hair, cream her face, and run, after a time, an expertly temperatured tub. After that she would read in bed.

Carol and Miles were alone in the living room. She sat beside him on the great couch patterned with spring blossoms and impossible birds and leaned her head against his shoulder. She said, "I'm so tired."

"I'll go soon," he told her, gently.

"No, stay, Miles, I've changed my mind — let's be married as soon as possible. Perhaps it could be arranged before Father goes overseas?"

Did it always happen this way, the saying of the right words at the wrong time? He cleared his throat and Carol drew away a little and looked at him. She asked, quickly, "What's the matter?"

"Nothing," he said. "Nothing. Only —"

"Only what?" she repeated, a little sharply. "Don't you want it — I thought — you said —"

He said instantly, "More than anything in the world. But I've been thinking. Ever since I was at the cottage, Carol. You were right, darling. It's best to wait."

She misinterpreted that, because she wished to, because it was imperative that she read a meaning into his words which would not possibly disturb her. She said, "Miles, your orders have come through!"

"No, dear," he said, "they haven't, yet."

"But you think — you've heard something?"

He shook his head, but she went on, as if speaking made it so, "You think they'll come too soon for arrangements here. All right, I can follow you and we can be married there, wherever it is — is that what you mean?"

He put his arm about her, and held her. He said, "Carol, it isn't fair to you. Ever since I knew about Pete . . . well, it's made me look at things differently. I can't put you through it. And I suppose," he added, "I've no right to ask you to wait. But I am going to ask you . . ."

"To wait?" she said incredulously, "you mean, until after the war?"

"That's it," he said.

She was silent a moment. Then she said, "But I don't understand."

He said, "I'll try to explain. Down there at the cottage, everything seemed pretty clear-cut and simple. Almost as if there were no war. We were in love, the thing to do was to get married. Then — Oh, good Lord," he said, "I sat up all night that night talking to Pete's wife. And today, you —

well, you saw what can happen."

She said scornfully, "Do you think that would change me? Do you think I'd be afraid? I would be, yes, every minute of the day, for you. But not for myself because we would have had something, Miles, we would have belonged."

He said, "Darling — it was you who wanted to wait. Remember?"

"Just so that you'd be *sure* —" She broke off, drew away from him, her eyes distended. She said, "That's it. You aren't sure. You never have been, except for that — that evening, in the cottage. So, it was just one of those things . . ."

"Carol —"

But she would not let him draw her close again. She repeated, "That's it. Well, thanks for letting me down gently." She got to her feet. She said, "Okay, Miles . . ."

He rose and stood looking down at her. He wanted to shake her until her teeth rattled. He did not touch her. He said, "You're making a mistake."

"You mean, I almost made a mistake. You almost made one, too," she said with bitterness, "but you woke up in time. Your leave's over, you're back at work, and you'll be going away soon. No entanglements, no complications, you've decided. That's best, isn't it?"

Her voice rose, a little. She said, "Down there at the cottage — you wanted to sleep with me, didn't you? And I wouldn't. Because I thought, we had the rest of our lives, long or short. I thought, we'd be married. I thought, let's not risk spoiling it. So because I wouldn't sleep with you, you said, 'We'll be married at once.' But I was a dope. I wanted you to be very sure. I was sure enough, for myself. But I couldn't be for us both —"

"Shut up!" he ordered. "You don't know what you are saying!" His face was white, and there was a whiter line around his mouth. He put out his hands and took her by the shoulders. Now he shook her, hard. When he released her, she stumbled and would have fallen if he had not reached out to steady her. He said, "You're a little fool. I'm in love with you. I want to marry you."

She said, "All right, then. We'll get the license, I'll have my blood test —"

He said, "No," heavily.

"It's either that," she said, "or goodbye."

"Carol —"

But she had turned away, she was walking out of the room. He heard her heels sound on the polished floor of the hall. He went out and stood at the foot of the stairs. She was half way up when she turned and looked down at him. She said, "Make up your mind."

She went on upstairs, steadily. On her mother's landing she paused and waited. She heard a door slam. The door slammed hard. There was no further sound.

Carol went into her mother's room. Helen was in the tub. She called, "Is that you, Carol? Come in."

The bathroom was very large. There were mirrors and a black and white and green decor. It was very becoming. Helen lay back in the tub, her red-gold head against a rubber pillow. The tray in front of her held jars, bottles, a magazine. The water foamed with fragrance. You could see her slender body through it, as through a veil. It was as straight and fine as a child's, the skin rosy, the contours preserved.

Carol sat down on a low chair by the tub. Helen said, "Miles has gone?"

"Yes." She looked at her mother. She asked, "Did you talk to him before I came in?"

"Well, naturally," Helen answered, in mild astonishment, "he was here for a few minutes. We didn't just sit and look at one another, darling!"

"Did you say anything about — our marrying?"

Helen picked up a sponge. She said, "Not very much. He said something vague about postponing it until after the war. It seemed a sensible measure to me, and I agreed."

"You didn't, by any chance, suggest it?"

Helen shrugged and the scented foam rippled. "I?" she asked, "my dear child, why should I? Where would it get me? You are both of age, you can do as you please. I've told you I didn't approve. That's as far as I can go. If you and Miles want to be married, you can be, tomorrow or next day or whenever it is convenient. I can't stop you. It would hardly make sense for me to try. I did try, as far as you were concerned. I didn't, with Miles. Opposition usually urges young men on. Give me credit for knowing that much. The last thing I would do, in the circumstances, is to try and persuade a soldier whose time is short that he should spend it in other ways than looking for a clergyman."

It was very convincing, all the more so because you would expect Helen's mind to work that way. Carol had seen it work that way a great many times. Besides, she thought Miles had been in the house only a few minutes before her arrival. Cocktails had been fetched at once, he was drinking his when she entered. There would not have been time for an important discussion.

She rose. She said, "Well, it's too bad you didn't try a little opposition — from my angle, that is."

Helen asked, casually, "You've decided to wait for the duration?'

"He's decided," said Carol, "I haven't. I'm not going to wait. We just won't be married, that's all."

She went out of the room. Helen adjusted the pillow more comfortably under her head. She thought, Well, that's that.

Miles would go away. Carol would eventually marry Dudley Lennox. Her life would follow a pleasant and ordered pattern, quilted with material prosperity. Dudley was a selfish man. He was not, Helen thought, especially fond of children. Carol was very young. Dudley would not make Helen Hillary a grandmother for some years, yet. Which, while a trivial consideration, was in the nature of a bonus.

Chapter Eighteen

Miles telephoned every day. Carol had returned to work, and he called her in the evening. She was not always at home. When she was she had one question to ask him. She would ask, "Have you changed your mind?" and when he said, "No, but I must talk to you, Carol, I must see you," she said, "Then it's of no use," and hung up.

For it seemed to her that things were singularly clear. He was not sure, or they would have been married by now. And if he were not sure what was the use of discussion? She had been an idiot to think that time made you sure. That's what she had thought, when she said at the cottage that they would wait a little while. What difference did a week, a month, a year, or a century make? Either you were sure, without reason, or you were not. It was like believing, it was like faith — it was like your belief in God, in the recurrence of spring, in the immortality of the human spirit. Either you believed or you didn't. Waiting didn't create belief, nor telling yourself that you believed.

His letters came and she read them. They said the same things, over and over, in as many ways as were possible to him. He was not very articulate on paper. They said that he loved her; he loved her enough not to wish her committed to constant anxiety and sorrow. He loved her enough to wait for her. Could she not say the same of him?

She did not answer the letters. She could not trust herself. She tried, she covered many sheets of note paper with her square, blunt writing and destroyed them. Because her pen had a life and a volition and a goal of its own, it ran away from her, it said things she would not say. It was a passionate and a humble pen. It asked, *Why?* It implored. It said, We are wasting our time.

You write at white heat, you seal and stamp the envelope and you go out and drop it in a letter box. And in due time it reaches the person for whom it is intended. His reading temperature is not, as a rule, your writing temperature — he reads it in the morning perhaps, after a bad night, too much to drink or too little sleep or anxiety over work. Or there's been an accident at the Field. Or he's lost at poker. Any one of a hundred things.

Or if, by a miracle, the reading temperature registers the same degree of fever, and he comes rushing to see you, as soon as it is possible. You don't want that. Temperatures, artificially induced, drop suddenly.

She thought, I'll talk to Father.

Adam was seldom at home these days, but she did find him in his study after dinner, one night. He was going through his wall safe and his desk, destroying papers. His clearances had come, and he was taking his shots, doubling up on them, looking and feeling wretched, in consequence. But things were breaking fast, Lennox wanted him in on the ground floor and he himself wanted to be there. He couldn't afford to spread the shots over a period of weeks.

His uniform had come, that worn by an accredited member of the Press at the battle front. And his equipment. His light, small typewriter, and the few things he would need.

"It's a clutter," he apologized, and grinned at Carol, "but find a place to sit down. Aunt Agatha was in a while ago. She wanted to help. I shooed her."

"Don't shoo me yet," said Carol. She found a place, and sat. She said, "I hate your going away."

"I hate it too, in one way," he said. "I wanted to see you and Miles married. You could have been, you know. By the time I

268

come back you'll be a settled matron. Or, rather, unsettled, a camp follower for the time being."

She said, leaning back in the big leather chair, "I don't think so."

Adam looked at her sharply. His head ached like hell and his arm was very sore. Also he had some degrees of fever. Things looked a little blurry to him. The room was very hot, as well, for he had been burning papers. He said, "My poor Perdon will faint when she sees this room. By the way, I'm keeping her on for a time. There's some stuff she can type and put in order for me. I've arranged to have her salary paid for as long as that takes, and as long thereafter until she gets another job."

His agent would look after Perdon. Oddly enough, she seemed the only person whom he must leave who needed looking after.

Carol said, "That's good," absently and Adam asked, "Hey, what's on your mind?"

She said, "You spoke of my marrying Miles. I don't think I'm going to."

Adam sat down at his desk. He said, "Good God, I never heard of such shilly-shallying. First Lennox, now Miles. What's gotten into you?"

She looked at him, with misery but resolution. She said, "I wish I knew. You see, he came down and stayed at the cottage with me —"

Adam drew a deep breath. His face did not alter. He asked, "So what?"

She smiled, faintly. She said, "It was all quite kosher. It might not have been — and in a way, I wish it hadn't . . ." She paused and went on, "But, it was. He wanted me to marry him as soon as possible. I thought, we'd better wait until at least he had his orders. I felt that he — might not be sure . . ."

"You were sure?"

"Yes," said Carol.

"Then, what?"

"I came to town," she said, "and Miles came up. In between seeing him one time and the next, he had changed his mind. He said it was because of Pete — you know, his friend, who is missing. He said we would wait until after the war."

Adam asked, "Does your mother know this?"

"I told her, that night."

"Had she talked to him about it?"

Carol said, "I was in Brooklyn. Miles got here just before I did."

Adam said, "Well?"

Carol made a small, weary gesture She said, "I think he's trying — to get out of it. I certainly won't stand in his way."

There was a pile of books on the desk. Adam flung them to the floor. The noise made his head worse and Carol jumped. He said irritably, "Sorry. Carol, I never thought you were in the least like your mother."

"Am I?" she asked.

"Or like me, for that matter," he went on. "I've always considered you something of a changeling and thanked God for it. But now you're turning out like us both. It's a pity. We're as muddle-headed a set of parents as you'll ever find. Your mother thinks around corners. Also she analyzes and psychologizes. I do, too. Partly because my trade is that of the novelist, and I have lost any talent for simple, direct thinking I ever had, through training for this trade. I stop to ask, why, when, how? I stop to wonder at your motives, question my own, doubt everyone else's. That's the way it is. It is a hindrance to living, not a help. Are you in love with this boy?"

"You know I am."

"You'd take your chances with him tomorrow?"

"Yes," she said and for the first time her eyes spilled over and her father looked away, angry and embarrassed.

He said, "And he's in love with you?"

"I thought so," Carol told him. "I don't know now if it's love or —"

271

He said, "If you start that 'just' business again, I'll forget you are twenty-three and put you over my knee and whale hell out of you. There's nothing I can do about this. It's up to you — and to Miles. I'm getting out of here. Also, I have my own problems. You wouldn't think I'd have them at my age, but I have. And you're going to listen to me, for a change. I haven't told your mother yet, but I shall. I want her to divorce me. I want her to go to Reno. And I want to marry Jenny. I should have done so long ago. Your mother persuaded me, when you were small, that it was for your best interest that we remain, at least outwardly, together. I dare say you know that by now. Later, when it seemed to me that you were sufficiently adult to take a parental divorce in your stride, she threatened to name Jenny as correspondent. Jenny was midway in her career. Granted that it isn't very important, as careers go, it meant a good deal to her. Granted, too, that scandal doesn't hurt an actress, it would have harmed her. Not as far as audiences and box offices go, but within herself, intimately. She's a good kid," he said, gently, and seemed to forget Carol was in the room. "She made a mistake when I came along but she's stood by it. There have been plenty of rumors, of course, and they have foundation

272

in fact. But no open scandal as long as your mother and Jenny appeared to be friends. Now it doesn't matter. She's going to tour the camps, she hopes to get overseas, and she isn't going back on the stage. As soon as I am free, we'll be married. And if your mother refuses," he added, "I shall divorce her, upon my return."

Carol said, after a moment, "It should have happened long ago."

"Thanks," he said. He added, "It's better now, perhaps. It won't hurt you. You have other things to think about. What happens to me or your mother or Jenny won't mean very much to you, Carol. Just what happens to you and Miles."

He stooped to pick up the books, and was dizzy. He said, "Ring for Ole, will you? He can give me a hand. I feel like the devil. I'm going to bed."

She rang and he straightened himself with an effort and walked to the door with her, his big hand on her shoulder. He said, "If I were you, I wouldn't throw away something you believe is worth keeping until I were sure I didn't want it."

She tried to smile and Adam bent and kissed her cheek. He watched the door close behind her. He waited for Ole, feeling ill and lonely. He wished Jenny were here. She could be very quiet, her small hands were cool and kind. She was the kindest woman he had ever known, the merriest, the most loving.

He tried to think about Carol. There was something very screwy there, he told himself, something which didn't add up, which didn't make sense. He thought, *and I bet it's Helen.*

But how? he wondered and was back again in the old pattern of puzzling things out, wondering what made people tick. How, and when, and why?

Adam Hillary's affairs were in order. If anything happened to him overseas Carol would have a legacy. He was not a rich man. Like most writers he had no capital but he had enjoyed a large income for some years. He had been very successful. He earned excellent lecture fees, and his novels had gone to Hollywood. He was also extravagant and generous. He was always good for a loan — rarely repaid — or a check to charity. The rising income taxes took a lion's share of his earnings but such investments as he had made were sound, and there was cash in the bank.

Helen wouldn't suffer. She earned as much as he, and would go on earning it. The house was in her name, and the cottage. She had invested more than he. One of her most devoted friends in the old days was a well known banker. Agatha Stuart had her own income. And Jenny's earning capacity was superior to Adam's.

He had made a new will, leaving small annuities to Miss Perdon, Ole, and Marta. Everything else went to Carol. His daughter could earn her own living. To be sure she made her home with her parents and her salary went for personal needs and spending money. Helen bestowed fur coats, jewelry, fripperies upon her with a lavish hand. But if she did not marry, if she wished to pull away from the Hillary household, Adam's money would insure her bed, board, medical care — and emancipate her from Helen's tendency to what Adam mentally termed, *lagniappe*.

If she married — well, the money would augment a Major's pay, assuming that she married Miles. He thought, I'd like to have a talk with the boy, and dismissed the idea. Even were it possible, it would be foolish. There was nothing he could say; or, rather, no matter what he said, it would make no difference in the long run. Whatever was right or wrong between them was their affair. He thought, I've been a damned failure as a parent — too absorbed in my own situation to give her more than a corner of my mind. You couldn't go along for twenty-three years on a live-and-let-live basis, easy and undemanding, and then suddenly, come all over the heavy father, the guide, philosopher and friend. Carol's infancy belonged to trained nurses, her childhood to Aunt Agatha. Helen had been a bright sunbeam, a shower of gold in the nursery, darting in, disappearing, leaving in her wake teddy bears, dolls with real hair, miniature pianos and beautiful handmade clothes. When Carol grew into awkward coltish girlhood, touching and lovely, her schools had taken her away, her interests had been friends, teachers, and boys. During this period her character had been forming, it was a chisel which, with slow, almost imperceptible strokes, revealed the woman she was to become. And, he reflected, from the time she entered her teens the antagonism between her and her mother had been made apparent. Helen could not brook a will as strong, or stronger, than her own.

Helen was making preparations to go to the coast. One of the major studios was going to film the story of her adventures. Fictionized, of course, the facts taken from the story which *Foresight* was to print and Frank Whitney to publish in book form. Helen was amusing about it. The film would include her earlier travels, the torpedoing, the blitz, and then the Chinese journey. The girl who would play her part was, at the most, twenty-five. But one of the conditions to her acceptance of a stupendous sum for the motion picture rights was that she was to be consulted on the writing of the script and, when the picture went into production, upon the actual shooting. She couldn't, she said, afford too many mistakes.

On the afternoon before his departure, Adam knocked on her study door. When he entered she was dictating to one of her secretaries, the other was typing furiously. Through the open door to the bedroom he could see Cresson sorting what looked like heaps of pastel clouds for packing. A small pert manicurist was assembling her tools preparatory to departure. Cresson had no time for manicures today.

Adam said, "I'd like to talk to you, if I may."

Helen raised an eyebrow. She looked at the devoted secretaries resignedly. They vanished. The manicurist scuttled out, not without a lingering glance at Adam, who was in her estimation a beautiful hunk of man, if a little on the elderly side.

Helen's study was air-conditioned. The

books glowed on the shelves, flowers were bright and fragrant. The photographs of the great looked down from the walls in approval. The fireplace was filled with white birch logs.

Adam sat down, opposite his wife. He said, "As you know, I am leaving very early tomorrow morning. I don't believe in farewells at dawn. Too demoralizing, with the departing voyager anxious to be off and the collective family making the usual drowsy gestures. So I thought we'd say goodbye now. I sha'n't be in for dinner, and if I understood you correctly this morning, you won't be either. I'll say goodbye to Carol and Agatha tonight."

Helen said, "Well, good luck. I still think you're being unnecessarily dramatic."

He said, "Possibly. But it doesn't seem so to me. I want to be in on this. I could have had a desk job in Washington. But I didn't want it. I can't fight, but I can get closer to it than Washington. But before I go, there are a few things we must discuss — under the head of unfinished business, I've made my will. Everything's in order. As soon as I have an address, you'll be notified. Also of my safe arrival." He smiled faintly. "If anything happens to me —"

"It won't," she said.

"I dare say you are right. Although war correspondents have taken something of a beating in this fracas," he reminded her. "Personally, I hope nothing does, as I have made plans."

"Would they interest me?" she asked, politely.

"Anything is possible," he said. "Helen, can you be direct and truthful with me, for once? Have you any affection for me at all?"

"None," she said.

"Good," Adam said, and she felt a stab, not of astonishment, but of anger. "That makes it simpler. I didn't think you had, but I had to be sure." He shook his head. He added, "When I think back, when I remember how much in love we were . . . ."

"You got over it, quickly," she reminded him.

"No. I came back from the war and did my best to adjust to the routine life of a university town. I thought it was what you wanted. We had a home, and then a child. But it wasn't what you wanted —"

She said, "May I remind you that it was you who left me, to tear around Europe, with the usual results?"

He said, "You wouldn't go with me. And when I returned I found you had made definite plans —"

"How could I go — with a small child?"

"You could have. Other children have survived their parents' peregrinations. Carol was a healthy child. I earned enough money at all times to provide you and her with a home wherever we were, with nurses, schooling — I think Carol would have enjoyed it. She has a capacity for enjoyment. But you couldn't bear to be Adam Hillary's wife. You had to be Helen Hillary."

"It's rather late,"she said, "to reproach me. Also you did so thoroughly, years ago."

He said, "One reason why you didn't want to leave America was Robert Howson."

Helen laughed. "Poor Bob," she said, "I haven't thought of him in years."

"Nevertheless," said Adam, "he was a factor. The first rung of the ladder . . ."

She said, "You are being absurd. Robert was twice my age and more. He was simply the first person who believed in me, and my potentialities."

"He was my senior," said Adam, "the best professor of English in the country. Also one of my closest friends, a man I admired tremendously." He paused, thinking of Robert Howson. Well, that got him nowhere. Few women, certainly not Helen, were worth the rupture of that friendship, the loss of the young, lusty hero worship.

He said, "When on my return we patched things up —"

"For Carol's sake," she said, swiftly, "and because I thought that we might still make a success of our marriage. But the habit of infidelity was too well rooted in you, Adam."

He said sadly, "A man goes where he is wanted. Curiously enough I have never considered you unfaithful to me. To be unfaithful connotes a certain amount of prior fidelity. Also, infidelity is usually expressed in physical terms. You were never faithful to anyone but yourself. And as for physical infidelity . . ." he moved his heavy shoulders impatiently, "I don't know, and I care less. Sometimes, I have wondered. You are essentially a frigid woman. Your only passions are of the mind. Cold flesh and a burning mentality. It's a wicked combination. If you have surrendered to any man, it was with malice aforethought and because you could not get what you wanted any other way. But I doubt even that. You are almost inhumanly clever. I would stake my last dollar that you'd welsh. You'd have excellent excuses, the sort which would send the average man reeling from your presence filled with the unhappy guilt of the remorseful, swearing he wasn't fit to breathe the air. I don't know what the excuses have been but I can guess. Loneliness and an unhappy married life had brought you to this temptation, perhaps, and something you could only term real love. But for your child's sake you must make the supreme renunciation. Wonderful," he commented, "and unholy. Which brings up —"

She said, "I shall not sit here and listen to this. When I think of you and your — your women!"

He said, "You flatter me. There were not so many. They were nice women for the most part, and kind and gay. They had warmth and reality and delightful flaws. Most of all they were, as you say, *women*. But I'm afraid you must listen. I want to talk about Carol."

"What about her?"

"Just this. I think you have interfered between her and Miles. I think it is due to you that they appear to have reached an impasse. I cannot believe," he said, "that you care very deeply for Carol. But if you do, you will regret this, Helen. Because if she ever finds out —"

She said, "I don't know what you're talking about. I haven't even seen Miles. And I never interfere. Carol's of age, she can do as she pleases!"

He said, "I hope she does. And one more thing. Years ago I asked you for a divorce.

You refused because of Carol. Or so you said. I have asked you since, after Carol was old enough not to be hurt. As a matter of fact, growing up in this hostile household has probably done her more harm than good. Certainly she has never had a sense of security. And I was too concerned with my own affairs to try to give it to her until too late. Any security she has from now on must come out of herself and from her own decisions. I have already told her, Helen, that I am going to ask you again — and that I intend to marry Jenny. She did not seem in the least bit shocked — on the contrary. The situation can't have been pleasant for her —"

Helen broke in. She said, "I didn't make the situation!"

"No? I think you did. Because you wanted the picture of yourself intact. Charming wife, devoted mother — and a career. You wouldn't admit any failure openly, and a divorce meant failure in at least one department of your life. You liked being Mrs. Adam Hillary as well as Helen Hillary. But you had to be both. I haven't done too badly myself. So we became a legend. Fabulous, almost unique in our fields. Distort the picture, ever so little, and the legend becomes commonplace."

Helen's face was drawn, almost ugly with

anger. She said, "The only terms on which I will divorce you would be an action in New York state, naming Jenny."

Adam waited a moment. Then he said, carefully, "We expected that, Helen. Jenny's willing — more willing than I. I suppose I dislike discarding the ego-warming cloak we call chivalry. Jenny's leaving the stage pretty soon — for good."

He rose. He said, "Think it over. There's another side to the picture. For the legend of the devoted mother can be marred by an action for divorce which readers of the tabloids would assume unpleasant for Carol. They'll ask, 'Why didn't she go to Reno?' That's what most women do who wish to spare their children public laundering of family linen."

The door closed after him. Helen stared at it, her mouth taut. Then she rang for her secretaries. Before they came in she managed to look herself, a little wan, a little misty. After all, she had just said goodbye to her husband.

Only they hadn't said goodbye.

Adam spent the early part of the evening with Jenny. He told her of his conversation with Helen. "Monologue, really," he said with a rueful grin. He added, "I don't know what she'll do. I admit I put the screws on.

It makes sense. A lot of people would wonder why, after maintaining a fiction all these years, she comes out with facts." He touched Jenny's dark hair with his big hand. He said, "Try not to worry."

"I shall worry," she said, and the tears raced down her cheeks. "Not about her. I don't care what she does. If only you'll come back, darling, and we can be together."

"I shall," he promised. "I'll make it up to you, Jenny."

Later that night he said goodbye to Agatha, who patted his shoulder with her spare hand and said, "I don't like goodbyes. We'll not say it."

He agreed, smiling, and then said abruptly, "I've asked Helen for a divorce, which she refuses unless the conditions are her own. A New York State action. I don't know what she'll do. I don't want you upset. You've been a tower of strength, and I'm deeply grateful to you. Also I'm fond of you. I think you know that."

She said, with some difficulty, "I understand, Adam, don't fret about me. Poor Helen . . ." She looked up at his slight exclamation and said, sharply, "I don't mean that in the usual sense. But she has so little. She doesn't know it, of course. I believe I am the only person in the world who is truly fond of her. You were in love with her, then for years you hated her. Carol began with the natural, unthinking affection of a child for a parent. It rarely stays at that level. It has to be earned as the child grows older. Helen didn't earn it. She tried to buy, or force it, and didn't succeed, Carol being what she is. But I have nothing to gain or to lose, from my niece. I have had her with me since she was a child. I haven't been able to do anything for her, since she married you. Or even before. I run her house, relieve her of responsibility, but that's all. But the habit of loving dies hard. I do not admire Helen," she said, "and I do not condone her. She is not an admirable woman. But I love her because I cannot help it."

Adam went from Agatha's room to Carol's. She was in bed, reading, waiting for him. He sat down on the edge of the bed. He said, lightly, "This is it. If you hear stirring around the house in another few hours I forbid you to do anything about it."

"I won't," she said, shakily.

He said, "I'll be back. There's just one thing . . ." he hesitated.

"What?"

"If anything unlikely should happen to me, will you tell Jenny yourself?" he asked. "I don't want her to read it in the papers and that's what would happen. There's still a lot of formality about the next-of-kin business."

"Don't say it," said Carol. She added, "All right, Father."

"Thanks." He rose and looked down at her. "I'll expect a lot of letters when I've an address. Also a cable if and when you decide to change your status and residence." He watched her face harden. He said, "And, a suggestion — if I were you I'd check with Ole on the time Miles came to the house the day you were in Brooklyn. Ole has a retentive memory."

He bent and kissed her and stood up. "Good luck," he said, "I wish you'd say goodbye to Miles for me. Maybe I'll be seeing him. Stranger things have happened. I don't pretend I'm sorry to go, except for you . . ." He added, silently, *and Jenny*. Better leave it unsaid. Carol would know anyway.

She said, "Wait a moment. Did you — speak to Mother?"

"No dice," said Adam, "or rather she thinks she's loaded them. I'm not astonished. I didn't expect her to take the first train to Nevada." He went to the door, turned and waved and was gone. Carol brushed the tears from her cheeks. There was so much she might have said and had not. During the last few weeks they had been closer than they had ever been. And now he was leaving her. She felt forlorn and sorry for herself. Then she shook herself mentally. It was just as well. She might have grown to depend on him. It was silly to depend on anyone. In the last analysis you have only yourself.

If she asked Ole, and Ole said Miles had been in the house for some time before Carol's return what would that prove? Nothing except that Helen had lied. But if she had lied, she had a reason.

Chapter Nineteen

Carol was at the hospital a few nights later when Miles telephoned. Helen, sitting in the drawing room with Aunt Agatha and Frank Whitney heard Ole taking the call. She rose swiftly, went into the hall and stood at the open door of the telephone room. She said, "I'll speak to Major Duncan, Ole."

She went in and closed the door. "Miles?" she said. "It's Helen. Carol's at the hospital . . .

Miles said, his voice heavy with disappointment, "I'm shoving off in the morning."

"Where?"

"Texas," he told her briefly. "I can get to town tonight for an hour. If I could see her? Can I 'phone the hospital?"

"My dear," said Helen, "she's not permitted calls." She didn't know if that were true or not, but it didn't matter.

He said, doggedly, "She gets home about ten, doesn't she?"

"As a rule," said Helen. "But not tonight. She's going out — she hasn't told me where — but it seems that she and Dudley are going on to a party of sorts."

He asked, "You're trying to tell me that she doesn't *want* to see me?"

"I'm sorry," said Helen.

"She's seeing Lennox again," he said flatly. "Well, that tears it. You might tell her I called."

She said, again, "I'm so sorry, Miles."

But he had hung up. Helen sat a moment at the little telephone table and then she went back to the drawing room. She said lightly, in answer to an inquiring look from Agatha, "That was Miles."

Better, in case Agatha's ears were as sharp as her own and had heard Ole say, "Major Duncan?"

She turned back to Frank Whitney. Frank was saying, "So you're off tomorrow."

"Priority and all," she said, "though I dare say they'll set me down at a whistle-stop and I can cool my heels waiting for a train."

He said, "I hope not. Well, 'phone me when you get there." He looked at Agatha and smiled. He said, "I am always anxious until she does. Nothing must happen to her. We've got a book on our hands. It has everything. You know," he told Helen, "I've been plenty worried. The Duncan manuscript, for instance, I thought you were slipping."

"I know," she said, remorsefully, "but I

did the best I could, Frank. Miles is a darling but so very inarticulate. It was a case of injecting as much life as possible into cut and dried facts. He's very reticent. He tells what he's seen and what he's done but you learn nothing of his inner experience, his mental and emotional processes. When I tried to use my imagination he stopped me. He said it embarrassed him," Helen concluded, using her imagination freely.

"Well," said Frank, comfortably, "I can understand it. But you've got the whole business, the feeling of flight, the feeling of combat, in your own book. Now if Duncan's had that."

She said, ruefully, "That's what I tried to put in it, out of my own experience, my talks with other fighter pilots — but he wouldn't have it. So," she shrugged, "it's a composite picture."

"It's a damned good one," Whitney told her. "Lennox will make a killing and so will we."

They were still talking when Carol came in. Ole admitted her and said, "Major Duncan called, Miss Carol. Mrs. Hillary talked with him."

Carol glanced in the living room. Agatha was no longer there. She saw Frank Whitney, a highball glass in his hands, sitting alone by the fireplace. She asked, "Where is Mother, Ole?"

"She went upstairs. Someone called on her private wire."

Carol asked, "Ole, can you remember the last time Major Duncan was here? I was in Brooklyn and came in later. Do you remember if he came in just before I did or much earlier."

Ole said, "I remember because when I let him in he said, 'I'm very early.' Mrs. Hillary was in the drawing room." He stopped and considered. If he were curious he did not show it. He added, "It must have been nearly an hour before you returned, Miss Carol."

"Thanks," said Carol, and went into the drawing room, and Whitney rose to meet her. "Drink?" he asked. "Helen said she'd be right down."

Carol took the drink he offered. She said, "Lord, it's hot. What a summer!"

"Why aren't you weekending at the cottage?"

"Oh," she said, "it doesn't seem worthwhile — just for weekends." She waited impatiently until Helen came downstairs and when she was in the room said, "Ole tells me Miles called."

"Yes," said her mother, "he was sorry to

miss you. He said he'd call again tomorrow night."

Carol thought, If he does, I'll ask him to come to see me as soon as he can. I'll ask him, point blank, if mother said anything.

But he did not call. The slow, hot days went by. Helen was in Hollywood and Adam had cabled of his safe arrival. Carol saw Jenny Davis. The show was closing after Labor Day and Jenny would be off to the camps. After that, if everything went as she hoped, overseas. They did not talk intimately — it was too difficult. They lunched together twice, and once Carol, taking an out of town school friend to the play, went backstage to see the star, and found Dudley Lennox there with one of his bigger advertisers. The suggestion was made that they go out to supper. Jenny begged off. She was tired, she said, the heat had gotten her down. She was very thin, her face was worn to a triangle by anxiety.

Carol's school friend was all for supper and a couple of attractive men, although the advertiser hardly came in that category. Short of making a scene Carol could not refuse. They made the rounds, ended up at the Stork. Afterwards Dudley and she dropped the girl and the fat, pleasant gentleman —

"Paunch and Judy," murmured Dudley —
at their respective hotels.

Driving toward the house, "Like old
times," said Dudley cheerfully. "And you
needn't push yourself through the side of the
cab. I'm not going to make love to you. What
do you hear from Duncan?"

"Nothing," said Carol.

"Is it out of order if I ask why?"

She said, "I'd rather not discuss it with
you, Dudley."

"Okay," he said amiably, "how do you like
your father's cables?"

She said, "They're fine."

"We think so, too." He added, "Have you
seen Helen's story?"

"No."

"I'll send a proof down to your desk," he
promised. "I think it's the best thing she's
done."

When they reached the house he went up
the steps with her. He asked, at the door, "Is
there any reason why we can't lunch together
now and then?"

"None," she said, "except that I don't
want to, specially. Goodnight, Dudley."

He said thoughtfully, "I could fire you, you
know."

"I wish you would," said Carol, "as I
haven't the energy to fire myself. And I can

always get another job."

"That's what keeps you on the payroll," he said. "Anyway, it's nice to know that you breathe the same air conditioning."

The proof was on her desk the next morning. Carol laid it aside until the lunch hour. She was not particularly interested. Helen had written several short readable books since the fall of France. And prior to that. She had always been politically and internationally minded. She had a great deal of information, because the best brains were at her disposal. The best brains are usually those of men and many men, despite their brains, are susceptible. Helen had collected political economists, foreign correspondents, prophets and historians for years.

Carol lunched alone, away from the *Foresight* Building. She was in no mood for companionship. Waiting for her ham on rye and a pot of tea, she withdrew the proof from its large envelope and glanced at it.

The sandwich came and she did not eat it. The tea turned to lye, and cooled in the pot.

This was Helen's story. It was neoned with great names, it glittered with excitement, a breathless headlong quality, it made light of hardship and discomfort, it even made a little fun of the writer. It said, in effect, Look at me, a foolish, middle-aged woman tearing around the world and loving it, yet worrying over lipstick and astringent when the bombs are falling all around me. It was such a pretty picture of such a pretty woman washing out lingerie in strange places, spraining her ankle at the wrong time, getting into jams and out again. A valiant woman, who took things as they came; who leaned out of windows and watched the bright fingers of searchlights until someone yanked her back into the room again; who heard bombs fall and shells whistle; who went walking with History; who sat in gardens and talked of war and peace with people who fought one in order to attain the other.

But it was more than Helen's story. It was the story of the men she had met, most of them anonymous — bomber pilots, pursuit pilots, fighter pilots. Men of the infantry, the artillery, the engineers. Helen got around. Suddenly she had become their interpreter. Especially that of the pilots. She knew how they felt when the Zeroes came all around the clock. She knew how they felt when they were alerted, when they sat in the Ready Room, the Briefing Room. She knew how they felt, when they were afraid and when they were furious with avenging anger, how they felt when a man they loved died, when a plane did not return. She knew — and she set it down.

Carol got up, paid her check and went back to the office. She picked up the telephone on her desk and asked if Mr. Lennox were in the building. He was not. She left her name. She said, "Will you ask him to call me here or at home?" She did not care what his secretary thought and she knew that his secretary was thinking plenty.

For this was Miles' book. All of the book which mattered belonged to Miles. For she had heard him say these things. Not perhaps as prettied up by rhetoric but substantially the same. The night at the cottage when they had talked so long and so late — for she had forgotten nothing. She had forgotten no word and no gesture since the night they had danced together and she had fallen in love.

These were things he had told her, and which he had also told Helen. But Helen had not put them in the book which would be published under Miles' name, "As told to Helen Hillary." Helen had saved them for her own book.

Carol took the proof home. She sat reading it again, waiting for the call to go through to the Field. The call came and after an interval she learned that Major Duncan was no longer there. He had been transferred.

She was unable to obtain further information.

She hung up, finally. She thought, If I write, it will be forwarded.

She thought, He did call. He called to say he was leaving. Mother talked to him. When I came in from the hospital, she *knew*.

The black anger which filled her was bitter and heavy. The anger of the betrayed. There was no other word for it. Helen had betrayed them both for her own purposes.

The telephone rang. The pages of what was literally proof scattered over the floor of her bedroom. She picked up the instrument, her heart hammering. It could be Miles. It must be Miles. But it was not long distance, it was a local call. It was Dudley Lennox. He asked, "You called me, Carol?"

She said, "Yes. I want to see you. Could you come here, tonight, after dinner?"

He said that, yes, he could come. He had an engagement but he would break it.

"Thanks," said Carol and hung up.

Agatha was out. It was her night at Red Cross. Carol dined alone and Ole clucked despairingly. The beautiful jellied Madrilene, the chicken aspic, the green salad, the raspberry sherbet went back to Marta almost untouched. Carol drank three glasses of iced coffee and smoked half a dozen cigarettes. She thought, *If my father were here —*

Pull yourself together. You've never asked his help and, rarely, his opinion. You can get along without him. You can get along without anyone, even Miles, if that has to be. Learn your lesson the hard way. Everyone stands alone. The learners try to shift the weight to someone else's shoulders and they succeed, in a measure. You weren't permitted to be a learner. Maybe it's as well.

It was pretty bleak, getting along without Miles. She had been learning that for some weeks now. But whether he wanted or did not want her, whether his alteration had been due to Helen or to some compulsion of his own, something had to be done about Helen's book. Carol said, to herself, her bastard book. For that was what it was. In some way it must be legitimized.

When Dudley came she was waiting for him. He came into the drawing room, looked at her and smiled. "Special dispensation," he said, "or royal summons?"

Carol did not smile. Her face was almost austere. She indicated the chair opposite. She said, "Sit down, Dudley."

"Listen is obey." He sat down, offered her his cigarette case. She shook her head. Her mouth was dry and parched from smoking. She said, "Drinks, at your elbow."

"Short snort," he murmured. He poured it, set it down without drinking, and glanced at the proof lying neatly stacked on the table. "What do you think of it?" he asked.

She said, "I think a lot of, and about, it. This isn't Mother's book. It's Miles'."

He asked, "What do you mean by that?"

She explained briefly, and he listened. He said, after a while, "Aren't you permitting your — interest in Duncan to influence you? He —" he shrugged, "he couldn't have written one line of that."

"No," said Carol, "but he is the source material. He doesn't know it. Perhaps he will never know it unless it is drawn to his attention. You haven't seen his book, Dudley. It's a nice, pedestrian job. Everything which could make it important has been left out. But it's turned up — here."

He said, "My dear child, what do you expect me to do?"

"You can talk to Mother," she said, "in Hollywood and suggest that she make acknowledgment, if only in a foreword."

"Impossible," he said, "as it's gone to press."

"Then, later."

"You think she'd agree?" he asked,

amused. "And besides, what have you to go on? I have no doubt that Helen can produce her notes for the Duncan book and that they'll check with the book itself."

She said, quietly, "I might have known you wouldn't help me." She looked at him, very directly. "Miles and I were to be married," she said, "when he got his transfer. He wanted to be, before, but I thought it best to wait. Not very long ago, he suddenly agreed with me, even to the point of suggesting that we wait until after the war. I don't believe that it was his idea, any more than this book is Mother's." She waited a moment. She said, "Miles has been transferred. He called to tell me so, but I wasn't home. I did not learn of the transfer until tonight."

"Where is he?" asked Dudley.

"I don't know," Carol said, "but I'll find out." She stood up. She said, "You could find out for me."

He did not move. He said, "Sure. I have plenty of contacts and in any case it would not be difficult. But I don't intend to try."

"I didn't think you would," she said.

He rose and looked at her. He said, "The more you fight the better I like it. You have plenty of spirit. It would be wasted on the hero. Heroes are a dime a dozen. You have implied that your mother has had a hand in recent events. Have you considered how it became possible? Do you remember Duncan's emotional plight when he first came to New York? Anything may have happened. You may have been a detour, a diversion. Or he may be suffering from an emotional hangover. I won't ask you what took place during your interrupted idyll on the Island . . ."

She had her hand on the bellrope. When Ole came, she said, quietly, "Mr. Lennox is leaving."

But he wasn't, not yet. He waited until Ole had gone to stand by the door, and then he said, "All right. I like it better this way. I never pretended friendship, Carol. That's not what I feel nor what I want. I've done everything I could to prevent you from making a fool of yourself — and me. You and your father," he murmured, "are after all, oddly alike — reckless, stubborn, quixotic . . ."

She said, "My father believes in me and Miles . . ." She broke off and stared at him, saw his faint smile. She said, "You sent him overseas, deliberately — not because you needed or wanted him but to get him out of the way!"

He said, "As a matter of fact he's sending

in better copy than I thought. I'm losing nothing. But it was, if you must know, your mother's suggestion."

He walked into the hall where Ole waited woodenly. He said, pleasantly, "Goodnight, Ole," and the door closed after him.

Carol ran upstairs. She burst into Agatha's room without preliminaries. Agatha leaned over and turned the switch of the electric phonograph and put down her novel. She asked, sitting erect in bed, her white hair in two short braids, "What's happened — have you heard from your father?"

Carol sat down. She said, "No."

"Well, tell me," said Agatha, impatiently.

Carol told her, from the beginning. She told her about Miles at the cottage, and of their plans. She told her what had happened, and what she believed had happened. She put the proof of the book on the bed. She said, "Perhaps you won't believe it, as you haven't heard him talk . . ."

Agatha listened. Telling took a long time. Then she asked, "What are you going to do?"

"I'm resigning my job tomorrow morning. I'll find out where Miles is. Then, I'll write him I'm on my way. But I'll go via Hollywood."

"Your mother won't like that," said Agatha. "Yet if what you tell me is true, she may be more or less prepared, I dare say Dudley is calling her now."

"I didn't think of that," said Carol, looking stricken. She rallied, quickly. "I'll think of something," she said.

"No doubt," said Agatha. "Want me to go along?"

"No, thanks, darling."

"Have you enough money?"

"Yes."

"If not, wire me. And, if you're to be married," said Agatha, "perhaps I can get there in time. If not . . ." she put out her bony hand, "you have my blessing."

Chapter Twenty

Carol telephoned Washington. Her mother had a friend there, a gentleman ranking high in the Air Corps, whose duties kept him at the capital. It was largely through him that her mother's various trips had been arranged. He was very grateful to Helen Hillary. He had not forgotten the time, years ago, when she came to visit on the post. She could have easily brought his career to an abrupt conclusion. But she hadn't.

He was uneasily astonished to hear from Carol, whom he recalled as a gangling little girl. He asked, once she had gotten past the secretaries on the magic of her name, "What can I do for you?"

Carol said, "It's for Mother, really. You may recall that she returned home at the same time as Major Miles Duncan and that they collaborated on a book? It appears that the Major had been transferred suddenly from Mitchel Field and Mother wants to know where he is stationed. She has to reach him. The book is going to press."

"I read," said the great man, "that she was in Hollywood."

"Yes. She left a number of unfinished things, this being one," said Carol. "I tried to find out myself, in order not to bother you — and she's so rushed — so I thought —"

He said briskly, "I'll call you back. Or shall I wire her?"

"If you'd call me?" asked Carol hastily. "She will telephone here later in the day. And then I can tell her."

They hung up with expressions of mutual esteem and Carol went about her urgent affairs. Transportation was hard to obtain. She went to the travel agency often used by her mother. There would be Pullman space on the Century for her. But getting to Los Angeles was another matter. Perhaps, if she would not mind, a lower berth?

She wouldn't.

The call came through from Washington. The great man's secretary had been able to locate Major Duncan in Texas, and gave Carol the name of the field.

"Well," said Agatha, after this was reported to her, "are you going to wire Miles?"

"Not until after I've seen Mother," said Carol. "I've thought it over. I have to be *sure*."

Agatha reflected that was what living in an insecure household did to you — more than anything else, you had to be sure. Carol's passion for the bare bones of truth, for absolute certainty, was an integral part of her life pattern. She could take nothing for granted. Most youngsters did. They took parental devotion and protection for granted. They fell in love and they took that for granted, too. Everything would be all right. The happy ending. Not Carol. Nothing in her past experience had convinced her that you could take anything for granted.

Carol went to Los Angeles. The travel agency hadn't been able to reserve hotel accommodations there but it couldn't matter, said the clerk, as her mother had an ample suite. He advised her to take box lunches from Chicago, wished her luck, and turned to the violent ringing of his telephone, a harassed man who wished that people would stay home if it cost him his bread and butter.

Carol had been to Hollywood before, in a drawing room on the Superchief. This was no drawing room. This was a lower berth. This wasn't the Superchief nor the Chief. This was a long, long train filled with soldiers, sailors, marines. People sat up in day coaches. Babies cried. There was a smell of oranges, sour milk, diapers, dust, and weariness in the car in which she traveled.

If anything could teach you not to follow your man half across the continent it should be this trip, thought Carol. Only it didn't. Discomfort mattered only to the vacationers; not to women who were concerned with war only as it affected those they most loved, whose entire beings were concentrated upon obtaining the outward consolation of loving — touch and nearness and embrace, no matter how brief the time. It was heartbreaking, it was insane, it had its special beauty.

And she was part of it. She was going to Miles. He had not asked her to but she was going. This time, if he sent her away she would know that he did not love her.

Getting out of the taxi, walking into the big hotel set in its lush, green, landscaped ground — flowers and shrubs, palm trees, vines, cottages, swimming pools — she looked like a carbon copy of herself. You didn't get out of a train like that, hours late, and appear as if fashioned from moonlight and dew. You hadn't stepped out of *Vogue*. You'd stepped out of something which was just short of a cattle car, yet with the most profound admiration for the railroads of the United States, which were doing a job three times bigger than any public utility can be expected to do, and doing it well — or better — than possible.

The desk clerk slid his eyes around at her when her turn came and asked automatically, "Have you a reservation?"

She said, "No, but —"

"I'm sorry," he said wearily, and wished he were home. Thank God he at least had a home — with his feet in hot water, and a Scotch and soda in his hand. "There isn't a —"

She said, imperiously, "I am Mrs. Hillary's daughter. Will you tell her that I have arrived?"

His manner changed. Helen Hillary's daughter? Damned if he'd thought she had one. Or one as old as this. He said cautiously, "Mrs. Hillary hasn't mentioned to us that she was expecting you."

You had to be cautious. People did the damnedest things just trying to find a place to sleep.

Carol opened her purse. She always carried identification. Aunt Agatha insisted on it. "Suppose you were run over?" she'd ask. She put the wallet on the desk and he glanced at it. He said, "Sorry, Miss Hillary, but you have to be so careful. The boy will take you right up."

The boy took her up. They rang but there

was no answer. The boy unlocked the door with a passkey. It was a pretty suite, a duplex, with living and dining rooms downstairs and two bedrooms and baths above. It was filled with flowers. Helen's typewriter stood on a desk. She did not travel with secretaries these days. She was very patriotic.

"Guess Mrs. Hillary ain't here," said the boy sadly. He liked seeing Mrs. Hillary. Also she was generous.

Carol tipped him. She called room service and found that it was possible to have tea. She went upstairs, where the boy had taken her bag. One room was unoccupied, the other showed traces of Helen, cosmetic case, more flowers, clothes hanging in the closets.

Carol took off her dusty frock, and put on a robe. After tea she would bathe and rest.

Helen came in an hour or so later. Carol heard her key in the lock, her feet on the short flight of stairs, her voice calling. She could not have moved if it had meant her life.

Helen came in. She wore a new frock, a printed linen, a big hat, and short gloves. She looked animated, a little tanned, and very well. She cried, "Carol — I couldn't believe it when the clerk told me — why are you here, what has happened? Why didn't you let me know?"

When Dudley had 'phoned her he had said nothing about the possibility of Carol's coming to Hollywood. He hadn't guessed. He should have, she thought, fretfully.

Carol said, "If I had let you know you would have had a sudden urge to go to Palm Springs or Mexico City." She sat up and swung her long legs to the floor. Then she said, "I'm on my way to Texas. I stopped off to see you."

"Texas?" repeated Helen. She sat down, and found that she was shaking. She thought, for once directly, *This is the show-down.* She had never expected it to come.

"Texas," said Carol. "Miles is there."

"Really?" said Helen. "I didn't know."

"I think you did," said Carol. "I think he called and when he found out I was out, he told you."

Helen said, "Aren't you being a little dramatic? Of course he called. I told you so. He said he would call you back."

"He said," corrected Carol, "that he was going to Texas."

Helen thought, She's following him, he'll tell her . . . She smiled. She said, "All right. So he told me he was being transferred. He didn't," she added sweetly, "demand that I tell *you*. If he had wanted you to know he would have called the hospital, or managed to get to town, or at least wired you, or called again. But he didn't. He wanted it this way. The easier way for you both."

It sounded plausible. Carol said, stubbornly, "I will not believe it." She added, "I've read your book, in proof."

Helen was silent and wary. This much she knew; Dudley had told her. She waited.

Carol said, in a tight, frozen voice, "It isn't your book — that is, the part of it that matters, the part which will get the good press, and the acclaim, the part which will sell it. The rest doesn't matter. You've written all that before — how brave you are under fire, and what fun you have talking to generals. But the new part belongs to Miles. It belongs in his book, not in yours. But you wanted it for yours. If you had written his book as it should have been written you would have been only the mouthpiece, the dictaphone . . ."

Helen said, "You are being absurd. I have my notes for Miles' book. Also my own notes, made before his was ever written."

"No doubt," said Carol. "Are you going to write a foreword to the book before Frank publishes it, acknowledging your debt —

and your co-author?"

"No," said Helen. Her eyes were brilliant with anger. She added, "You are making a fool of yourself over a stupid, unimaginative boy who doesn't care enough for you to let you know where he's going. And if you go to Texas he'll tell you so!"

Carol said, "I'll take my chances on that. I'll also take him the *Foresight* proof."

"And what will that get you?" asked Helen.

"Nothing, probably," said Carol. "I didn't expect you'd make the acknowledgment. And I doubt if Miles would want it. It would only embarrass him. But, I thought I'd give you your chance, too."

Her mother asked, "Where is he, exactly?"

Carol laughed. She said, "I have no intention of telling you. You'd wire or telephone, you'd manage something, somehow."

Helen said, "It doesn't matter. I can find him."

"If you call Washington," said Carol casually, "you'll be in an awkward position. Because that's how *I* found out. I said I was calling for you. And so, got the information."

Helen commented, with a spark of admiration, "That was quite clever of you, Carol."

Carol said, "I thought so. I don't like being

clever. I don't like using — hereditary methods."

Helen rose. She said, "This has been a very interesting conversation. But I am dining out. We'll continue it, in the morning."

Carol shook her head. She said, "I sha'n't be here. I stopped in the station and bought my ticket, before I came to the hotel. I'll be gone before you get back. It's a slow train but it will serve." She rose and walked over to her mother. She said, "I don't know why you've done this, Mother — I don't know why you have been so opposed to my marriage or why you have used very curious methods to prevent it."

Helen still had the card which she had played one evening not so long ago. It had taken a trick once, it might again. This was a different game but it was a good card. She said, quietly, "I opposed your marriage, at first, because I felt it was not suitable and that you wouldn't be happy. I knew Miles before you did." She smiled. "And, I think, better." She let that sink in. "Later, I opposed it because I felt that after your absurd behavior in permitting Miles to come to the cottage when you were there, alone, you had created a situation. Men of Miles' type," she said carelessly, "are apt to cling to a code which is somewhat outmoded. I tried to persuade him that you were adult, that you knew what you were doing —" She broke off. She said, "I'm sorry. I didn't mean to say that."

"You meant it," said Carol, who was perfectly white. "But I don't believe you. When I see Miles, I'll believe him."

"Don't you think," asked Helen softly, "that you are recreating the same situation by pursuing him — unasked?"

"Possibly," said Carol, "but I don't care."

She waited a moment. Then she said, "I'll have some dinner downstairs and I've already asked for sandwiches and fruit to take with me. And for my bill . . ."

"Your bill?" repeated Helen, startled.

"Tea," said Carol, very matter of fact. "The sandwiches. I'll pay for dinner."

Helen's eyes filled, suddenly. She said, "Carol, aren't you carrying your — enmity too far?"

"You mean, what will the hotel people think?" asked Carol brutally. "They haven't time to think and it doesn't matter to me if they find time."

She watched Helen sit down again. She watched her cry. She remembered the night she had seen her cry in Miles' arms. Helen spoke, after a while, brokenly, "I — I have always acted in your best interests. Darling," she said, "if I have hurt you —"

"It's too late," said Carol. She said it sadly. She felt her sorrow. It was sorrow for loss, the loss of something she had never had.

It mustn't be this way, thought Helen frantically. The legend was fading, the beautiful picture dissolving. You couldn't prevent it. "Where is your charming daughter?" they would ask. What did you reply? "I haven't the faintest idea, as she hasn't chosen to tell me"?

She said, "All right. I — I did know Miles was going to Texas. He asked me to tell you. He wanted to come to town, at once. I said you — were out — with Dudley Lennox."

Sometimes honesty turns the trick, clears the atmosphere.

"I see," said Carol. "And what else?"

Helen said, "That day you were in Brooklyn, he came to the house. Early. I tried to convince him that it would be better if you waited until after the war."

"How?" asked Carol, evenly.

She answered evasively, "The usual arguments, all of them sound."

Now, Carol was dressing, rapidly. Her mother watched her; watched her comb and brush her hair, watched her powder, watched her use her lipstick. And then, saw her turn.

"Are you going to give Father his divorce?" she asked.

Helen said, "So he told you? Of course not. Unless he consents to a New York State divorce, naming his mistress."

Carol said, "I don't think your public would like that. It seems so — unsportsman-like."

Her mother said furiously, "If, when he comes home, he goes to Reno, I shall contest it, Carol."

"I don't know much about the law," Carol said, "but there must be a way in which I could help." She looked at her mother, thoughtfully. She said, "Even if it weren't a help legally, it wouldn't hurt *him* if I testified for him."

"You wouldn't dare!"

"I'd dare," said Carol unemotionally. "You don't want him, Mother. You haven't for a very long time. You never wanted me. We — Father and I — we were just part of the picture. We made such a — rounded portrait. But we're out of the picture now, no matter what you do or don't do. So, it would be more sensible to pattern what you decide to do on that, wouldn't it?"

She put her things in her suitcase, locked it. She said, "I'm going now." She looked at her mother. She added, "I'll let you know, of course, what we decide. Goodbye — I wish it could have been different. But things don't alter in ten minutes, after twenty-three years."

She was gone, walking down the stairs, carrying her suitcase, her head very high. Helen could not see that her chin shook and her mouth was twisted and her eyes wet because it was so miserable an ending, and so inevitable. She ran to the stairs, she looked down, she called, "Carol, *Carol . . . !*" but a door closed and there was no answer.

Helen went into her bedroom. She stood for a long time and looked in the mirror. She was still lovely, and she was not yet fifty. But she would be.

She was alone.

Carol had tied her hands. There was nothing she could do and preserve face. There was only one thing possible. To go to Reno, when the arrangements had been made and Adam notified, and get her divorce with as much dignity as possible. Because any scandal would react, not on Jenny, not on Adam, but on her. People would talk, at the Stork, at Ciro's, at Victor's; people would talk at beach clubs, in Newport, at the Ritz, at the Algonquin; people would say, "But even if everyone *knew* that he and Jenny Davis lived together — there must have been something very fishy in that household if Helen Hillary's own daughter would —"

She shuddered, thinking of that.

Well, there were ways out. A quiet divorce, a gallant stand for the press. The wronged, but never the avenger. She'd been through blitzes before. There wasn't an ounce of physical fear in her. That much was true. She'd take this other kind of blitz too. She could turn it to her own advantage. She had always been an opportunist

She thought, with anger and unwilling admiration, Carol's like me, after all.

So she was. She had something of them both; Adam's stubbornness, his logic, his reckless emotional compulsions. She had an echo of her mother's wit and fluidity and determination. She possessed her mother's weapons also, because most women have them, if few know how to use them with reason. But what she had from her parents she had made her own, and her integrity shone through.

Helen thought, I'm not *beaten.*

She wasn't. There were years ahead of her. There was more success, adulation, flattery. There were wonderful dressmakers and plastic surgeons. There were other men. There were lots of men.

She sat down at her dressing table and

looked in the mirror. What she saw frightened her and she put her face in her hands and wept. These were real tears. It was a pity that Carol was not there to see them.

Chapter Twenty-One

Carol wired Miles from the station. She said, "I am on my way." She added the time her train might be expected and the name of the hotel to which she was going. She had asked for a list of the hotels at the Travelers Aid desk. She had wired the hotel they recommended.

She did not sleep that night. She did not rest during the dusty trip, the many stops, the repetitive pattern, soldiers, wives, mothers and babies. She was thinking ahead, she was running, fleetly, in advance of the train. She was thinking of Helen. She thought, I never loved her, and she was more unhappy than if she had. She had believed for so long that what she felt was love — now she knew it had never been, not since she was a small child, loving everyone and the world, as all children do, for a little while. What she had mistaken for love was a lesson each child learns by rote. They learn — this is your mother, this is your father, they are your parents, therefore you must love them.

Fortunate children eventually learn, by heart. Fortunate children grow naturally into loving. Sometimes parents earn this and sometimes they do not.

She thought, If Miles and I have children I shall love them so much, for his sake and for my own, but most of all for theirs. And perhaps they will love me in return. She was humble, thinking that. She thought, If they know they are safe with us, if they understand that they can count on us, if they feel themselves secure.

There is no other security. Money does not buy it; anything can happen to money. Environment does not assure it; environment can alter overnight. But the warm, wide, selfless loving — this is all the security any child needs, or any adult, for that matter, to take him safely through the difficult and exciting, the heartbreaking and wonderful moment called living.

No one met her at the crowded, echoing station. It was terribly hot, it was windy, dust choked her and seeped in her pores. She waited a long time for a taxi and finally shared one, which took her to the hotel. It was a big place and it was crowded. They had had her wire, but they were unable to accommodate her. Perhaps by late tonight, if she cared to wait?

She would wait. This was where she had

told Miles she would be and where he would find her. She did not dare risk going out and searching for another place. The clerks were so busy, so haggard, they might forget to tell him where she was, even if she found a place and could telephone.

She would not call the Field. He had her wire, eventually he would come.

She waited in the lobby. She had something to eat in the coffee shop cafeteria, she went back to the lobby and waited. She wired Aunt Agatha. She bought a paper. She watched people. Hundreds of people. Chinese, Mexican, American. Uniforms with wings. The wings of a command pilot, the wings of a senior pilot, the new wings of a recently graduated cadet. She looked at shoulder bars. She looked at faces. She saw cattlemen and cowboys. She saw pretty women. She saw schoolgirls. She saw prostitutes.

It was dark before he came. She was still sitting there patiently. But a moment before he pushed through the revolving doors, she had dropped off to sleep. She sat in a big, dusty plush chair, her suitcase beside her, her hat on her suitcase. Her dark, disheveled head was against the back of the chair. Her face was white and quiet, and her heavy lids were folded down secretly over her eyes. Her mouth was very red and young.

He stood beside her and experienced a tenderness so nearly unbearable that he felt he must weep.

He said, urgently, "Carol . . ."

She sighed, opened her eyes and looked at him. She did not stir. She looked and looked, and presently she smiled.

He said, "You crazy little . . . !" He stopped, and went on. "I came as soon as I could," he told her. "I've been away from the Field. Otherwise I would have met you, if possible, or sent someone, or wired — but I got back less than an hour ago and found your wire."

"It doesn't matter," she said, "you're here now."

He picked up her suitcase. "Come on," he said.

Carol rose. She was giddy with fatigue. She said, dizzily, "They said I might have a room here, late tonight, if I waited."

"The hell with that," he told her. "You're coming with me. Jim O'Connor's my C.O. I knew him way back when. I talked with his wife before I came into town. You're going there. They live off Post and there's plenty of room."

He had her arm. *How thin she was.* He took her out and put her in an army car. She said, shakily, as they made their way through traffic, "I don't know, Miles, I have so much to say and somehow I can't say it. I feel funny," she said like a child, "all sort of gone and queer inside."

"It will keep," he told her. "Here, lean back, close your eyes."

When they reached the pleasant house of the O'Connors he had to lift her from the car. She was nearly asleep again, she dragged against him as he half-carried her up the walk. Mrs. O'Connor met them at the door. She was, Carol saw dimly, a pretty woman in her forties. She looked at Miles and at Carol. She said, "Here, give her to me."

Between them they got her upstairs, and into a small guest room. And Miles said anxiously, as if Carol could not hear, "I don't know what's the matter with her. It can't be just because she's tired."

Mrs. O'Connor had been a trained nurse. She said, "I don't know either, but it looks like some sort of shock or emotional reaction. Clear out," she ordered, "I've work to do."

Carol remembered very little, afterwards. She knew she was somewhere, and that Miles was not far away. She knew she was in bed, with fresh sweet linen under and over her, and a clean nightgown on her tired body. She knew that she had been washed and her hair brushed and given something that fizzed in a glass. She knew that it was an effort to move or to speak, and that the woman who was in the room with her told her she need not try to do either. She was very grateful. She said, "Miles?" and went to sleep.

She woke to sunlight and a blue sky, and to see the dusty green of cottonwoods beyond her windows. She heard a child's laughter, and an older child saying, "hush" and her door opened quietly and Mrs. O'Connor stood there with a tray in her hands. She asked, "Are you awake and hungry?"

Carol sat up. "I'm starved!" she said. "I — what happened to me last night?" She looked, flushing, at the older woman. "What must you think of me?"

Mary O'Connor said briskly, "I think you've had a hard trip and a shock somewhere along the way. I think you're very pretty now that you've rested, and almost good enough to be Miles' girl."

Carol's color deepened. She said, eating bacon and eggs and drinking the strong, fragrant coffee, "I can never thank you . . ."

"You passed out," said Mrs. O'Connor

cheerfully. "I believe you've been on a bender — I'm not talking about alcohol," she said, smiling.

Carol said, "The trip wasn't too bad — I stopped off for a few hours in Hollywood. Things have been happening pretty fast . . ."

"They always do, these days."

"What time is it?" asked Carol.

"It's noon. My kids are home and clamoring for food."

"I'd love to see them," Carol said, "if I may." She looked at Mary appealingly. "I — this is such an imposition."

"No," said Mrs. O'Connor. "It's for Miles. For you, too, now. Jim and I have a son," she said, quietly. "He's a fighter pilot. He would have been shot down on his first mission if it hadn't been for Miles, who got there first and shot the enemy down instead. Jim Jr. lost a lot of plane, and had a hole in his arm and one in his leg, but he landed, he was alive, he still is. We — think a lot of Miles," she said.

At the door, she turned. She said, "Try to rest. I'll let you up for dinner. Miles can't be here till afterward. I suggested taking you out to the Field and eating, all of us, at the Officers Mess, but he said, No, he'd be in later and see you. Jim won't be home till then either. If you don't mind kids, we'll have dinner with them, if you can take my cooking. I haven't had a maid since I came."

Carol slept most of the day. Then she got up, bathed and dressed, and they had dinner. The little girl and the older boy were noisy, natural and charming. Carol helped dry the dishes. When the doorbell rang Mrs. O'Connor shooed her out into the hall. "You take him into the living room," she said. "I have things to do."

Colonel Jim O'Connor was with Miles. Carol had an impression of a tall man with a brown face and graying hair, a wide smile and very blue eyes. He took her hand, held it a moment and vanished as if by magic. The children had gone, too.

The living room was very quiet. It was not a notable room. This was a rented house, and not much of the O'Connor personality went into it. But it was a room Carol would always remember.

"You feel all right?" asked Miles. He had not touched her.

"I feel fine. I —" she laughed, "I was sponged and pressed and put to bed. I'm sorry I went all swooning and collapsing on you, Miles."

He said, "You look — okay." He sat down on the couch and after a moment she went to sit beside him. He asked, "Why did you come?"

"To beg you to marry me."

"Carol —" he looked at her, shook his head. "I — you know how I feel —"

"Do you, Miles? Do you really feel that way?" she asked earnestly. "No, look at me. You see, I've seen Mother in Hollywood. She told me — under some pressure — that you had 'phoned and said you were being transferred. I was at the hospital. I didn't go out afterwards with Dudley. I had no date with him. I came home, early."

He said, "But why . . . ? That was a deliberate lie."

"Yes." She was grave, and stern, telling him how deliberate. "She told me when I came in that you had telephoned and would call again. She did not say your orders had come — and there's something else. My mother said — that one reason she opposed our marriage was because — of your coming to the cottage — she felt that you might think that because we had been exposed to gossip, which in this case was Dudley — you would feel under obligation."

He cried, "She told you *that?* But it was in reverse, Carol. When we talked together that day while I waited for you, she said that a hasty marriage could have only one implication. That it was necessary. She asked me, was that why I was so insistent?"

Carol said, between laughter and tears, "So that was it! I wondered at the time if she had said anything, if she had discussed it with you. She said, when I asked her, No, as you were there only a few minutes before me."

"Well, by God," said Miles and drew a deep breath. "And all the time I thought —"

"That you were protecting me?" She smiled. She said, "It's out in the open now."

"But I don't understand," he said, bewildered, "I thought she — liked me. I mean, why would she do such a thing? She — she's your mother," he said angrily. It was hard to dispel the magic. He said, "It's difficult to believe."

Carol said, evenly, "She cares for no one but herself. Miles, your book. The best of it. The things you must have told her, from the first day you met and afterwards. The things you told me, at the cottage. They aren't in your book, darling, they're in hers — I have the proofs. I asked her if she would make an acknowledgment, when her book is published. She said no. She denies everything, naturally. And we have no proofs," she added, "and I'm not trying to make a bad pun!"

He stared at her a moment, thoughtfully.

330

He didn't care about the book. The book had been an excuse to be with Helen Hillary. He admitted that. She could use him for a hundred books and he wouldn't care now. But the fact that she had used him, that was different — that was the payoff, that was the works.

He said, "To hell with the book. When I think what she's done to us . . ." He swore, fluently, stopped. "I'm sorry," he said.

"You needn't be. We're — washed up." She added, "It was Mother who suggested that Dudley send Father overseas. She thought he was an ally. And he was, he is."

Later she could tell him the rest, show him Helen's book, fill in the details, tell him about Adam and Jenny. But not now. She asked, "Shall I go back?"

"And leave me? Never again." He took her in his arms and kissed her, for the first time since they had been together. He kissed her with tenderness and exaltation and hunger. He said, "Wire Aunt Agatha and get her here if you can. If not, Mary O'Connor will stand by. We'll cable your father. I may not be here long, darling, but we'll find a place somewhere if it's over a garage or in a motor court or a shack. Will you mind?"

"I won't mind," she said, close in his arms.

"The arrangements won't take too long,"

he said, "and the Chaplain will marry us. And then we'll be together for as much time as there'll be left."

"However short," she told him, "it will be forever, and however long it will seem too brief. Miles, we're on our own," she said, "you and I — we're a *family*."

That was it. All the family she had, really. Agatha loved her but she was old, and of another generation, another way of living and of thought. Adam loved her, but when he came back he would have Jenny, they would make their own lives, they too belonged to another generation Helen had never been part of her family, she belonged exclusively to herself. They would patch it up perhaps, see one another occasionally, some day, pay lip service to their purely biological relationship. Helen would see to that, for the sake of the legend. But that door had closed — if ever it had been open. Unlocked, Carol thought, on my side only, and not for very long.

He asked, anxiously, "You're not afraid? A good many of the things Helen said to me are true enough, God knows — the worry and the heartbreak and the risks . . ."

"Oh be quiet," she said, and kissed him with honesty and ardor, "we have each other, and we have today."